REBELS WEST!

Also by Jack Cummings

Dead Man's Medal
Sergeant Gringo
Lynch's Revenge
Tiger Butte

REBELS WEST!

Jack Cummings

COPY 1

Walker and Company
New York

First published in the United States of America in 1987 by the Walker Publishing Company, Inc.

Published simultaneously in Canada by John Wiley & Sons Canada, Limited, Rexdale, Ontario.

Library of Congress Cataloging-in-Publication Data

Cummings, Jack, 1925–
    Rebels West!

    1. United States—History—Civil War, 1861–1865—
Fiction.   I. Title.
PS3553.U444R4 1987   813′.54   86-24726
ISBN 0-8027-0943-5

Printed in the United States of America

10 9 8 7 6 5 4 3 2 1

AUTHOR'S NOTE

Three and a half years of civil war against the South had drained the western frontier forts of Union soldiers, leaving the settlers nearly defenseless against the marauding Indian tribes.

By 1864 the U.S. War Department turned in desperation to those captured Confederate soldiers rotting in the prisoner-of-war pens at Point Lookout; Rock Island; Alton; Camps Douglas, Chase, and Morton; and asked for volunteers to man the outposts.

Ill-fed and ill-treated, some of these southerners exchanged their tattered gray uniforms for the hated Union blue, and went west, hoping to escape their misery. They became known as Galvanized Yankees.

PROLOGUE

MAY 1866.

THE major, a staff officer from the War Department, his tailored blue uniform powdered with travel dust from the stage run across Kansas from Fort Leavenworth, stared down at the burial marker.

The Smoky Hill Route stage station, which bordered the eastern edge of the town of Cheyenne Springs not far into Colorado Territory, seemed a strange place to find the headstone of the man whose disappearance he had been sent to investigate.

"You do not have a regular cemetery, ma'am?" he said.

Esther Searle, wife of the station keeper, who had led him to the grave site, said, "Oh, yes, Major Ronstadt. It's at the other side of the town."

She said it casually. Too casually, was the major's first impression. But he was hot and tired and looking forward to the comforts of Denver, and he was willing to consider her explanation.

"It was my own pleading that got him buried here," she said.

He was surprised to see quick tears come to her eyes.

"He was our protector," Esther said. "A hero to us all. It seemed that what he did for us . . . deserved more than just a plot in the town's Boot Hill." She paused, then went on. "It was here he fought off the first Cheyenne attack, right here on the station. Then later, twice, he saved the town. The last time from extinction."

She gestured around at the station grounds. "Here, where

1

travelers come and go, they can be shown this memorial, even those who did not have the privilege of knowing him."

The major read the epitaph, carefully carved on the fine, large chunk of polished granite:

CAPTAIN JUSTIN RHETT, C.S.A.
1835–1865
With Eternal Gratitude
from
The People of Cheyenne Springs

The Union officer frowned. "C.S.A. Confederate States Army. That is incorrect, ma'am. Decidedly incorrect. At the time he was on duty here, he was a sergeant of the Union Army. A Galvanized Yankee, to be precise."

"Of course. We knew that."

"Then why—"

"It seemed more suitable this way. It fit the man better, Major. Fit the circumstance better, we felt."

"Possibly I can understand your feeling," Major Ronstadt said. "Even though my information is that you people here were staunch Union supporters throughout the war."

She said, "Which makes what he did even more heroic, him being a southerner, don't you see?"

"And his men?" Ronstadt said. "What happened to them?"

"We never knew, sir. They just rode away afterward, and nothing was ever heard of them again."

"Deserters!" the major said.

"Possibly," the station keeper's wife said. "But they all fought heroically beside him when the Cheyenne attacks came."

"If caught, they will all be shot," the major said. "As they deserve."

Esther Searle said nothing. She had no wish to provoke an argument with the Union officer. It was best to get rid of him as soon as possible, she thought.

She had never been good at lying.

CHAPTER 1

AUGUST 1864.

HE had driven the wagon with the ton of gold bullion hidden under a false bottom, pulled by a six-mule team, all the way from the Clear Creek, Colorado, mining district.

It was gold for the Confederacy, gathered over many months by a secret group of southern sympathizers, part of the Copperhead conspiracy. It had been gathered in ways he did not care to think about. That was not his concern.

He was Justin Rhett, captain of Confederate Cavalry, out of uniform in enemy territory, and his sole concern was to deliver the half million dollars in gold bars to General Sterling Price in Arkansas. Price needed it urgently to properly arm and equip the army he had poised to invade the North, in a desperate attempt to save the South in this, the fourth, year of the War of the Rebellion.

And now, within patrol range of Fort Lyon, Colorado Territory, he feared that his stretch of luck could run out. Although the frontier forts had been drained of Union Army regulars by the need for troops to fight the rebels, there were, here and there, detachments of Territorial Volunteers remaining.

His fear, as it had been from the beginning, was that he would be confronted by one of these.

And even as he thought about this, it happened.

Ten soldiers in blue rode up, led by a sergeant about Rhett's own age. Thirty, Rhett guessed, and with a face tempered tough by something more than wind and sun.

"Where you headed?" the sergeant demanded.

"Figure to cut the Santa Fe Trail up ahead," Rhett said, trying to sound easy.

"Where from?"

"Been working at the mines up Colorado way."

"You're still in Colorado. I'll ask again. Where from?"

Rhett barely hesitated. "Around the Clear Creek diggings."

"Damned heavy wagon," the sergeant said. "What you hauling?"

"Nothing now. Just my possibles and feed for the team."

"You would have done better to sell the rig and buy yourself a saddle horse and pack mule."

"I kept it for a reason. Figure to do some freighting along the trail."

"Damn wagon looks heavy enough to haul ore."

Rhett nodded. "Fellow I bought it from, done some of that." Then, to change the subject, he said, "How far to Fort Lyon?"

"About thirty miles."

"Any Injun trouble hereabouts?"

"Some. Handful of Cheyenne hit a Mexican freight train on the trail a few days back. Stole all the whiskey they could carry off, and killed a few Mex doing it. We think they headed north this way, is why we're on the scout. Injuns and whiskey can spell big trouble. You better hope they don't run onto you traveling alone."

"I appreciate your warning, suh," Rhett said.

The sergeant scowled. "Southerner, ain't you?"

"Texan," Rhett said.

"You damned Johnny Rebs would do better to stay down where you belong."

"All us Texans ain't secesh," Rhett said. "There was some of us wanted to stay in the Union."

"So *you* say. Me, now, I ain't inclined to believe that."

Rhett didn't think it was wise to act too meek. He said, letting his voice harden, "You wouldn't call a man a liar?"

The sergeant met Rhett's steel-gray eyes for a long moment. Finally he said, "I reckon there are exceptions."

Rhett gave a short nod.

After a pause, the sergeant said, "Any Injun sign on your way down?"

"None."

"Might be they didn't keep on north. We may turn back if we don't sight the bastards. If we do, we'll keep an eye out for you."

"I'd appreciate that, suh."

"You got a military look about you, damned if you ain't," the noncom said. "Do they 'sir' the sergeants in the reb army?"

"Couldn't say," Rhett said. "I've always been a civilian." He paused. "Are you regular army, suh?"

The sergeant studied him before he answered. "No. We're Colorado Volunteer Cavalry. Part of Colonel Chivington's command."

"Well, thanks for your warning, suh," Rhett said. "About the Injuns, I mean. With your permission, I'll be on my way."

"Go ahead," the sergeant said. But his eyes continued to probe.

The country here was mostly sloping grassland, but ahead he knew was a stretch of rougher land, cut here and there by storm runoff. He remembered it from when, several weeks before, he had ridden the same route on his way from Arkansas.

He intended to skirt east of Fort Lyon toward the Kansas border. Once he crossed the Arkansas River he'd strike directly for the Cimarron Strip and turn east through the Territory of the Civilized Tribes. He still had a long and hazardous way to go.

The team plodded onward, while he thought back on the origin of this mission he'd been sent on by General Price.

He hadn't known if the idea had originated with "Old Pap" Price, so-called because of his white hair, or with some superior. But it was Price himself, he'd heard, who had selected him.

A colonel named Joshua Falk was the one who laid it out for him. "You're the man we want," Colonel Falk had said. "We understand you scouted for the U.S. Army out of Fort Union before the rebellion started and you resigned to enlist in the Texas Cavalry. So you know the frontier, and you know something of Indians."

"Comanche, Kiowa, some Apache, mostly, suh."

"Cheyenne?"

"Southern Cheyenne, some, suh."

"Still qualifies you better than any man we have knowledge of," Falk said. "Of course this is a volunteer mission. Behind the lines into Colorado. If you are caught—well, you know what would happen."

"How important is it to the South, suh?"

"It could save us from losing the war," Falk said. "Here, on the western border, at least. We are planning a strike up through Missouri, and if we have money to properly equip ourselves, we'll turn west and drive clear across Kansas. That could be a severe setback for the North and a great boost for the South." He paused. "As you must know from your own observation, we are presently ill equipped for such an action. Our troops in the main theater to the east have had first grab on what is available. We need gold to do this right. And we need you to get it."

Rhett's reminiscing was abruptly interrupted as his eyes caught a plume of rising dust off to his distant right. It appeared to be coming toward him. Another patrol?

Possibly. The sergeant had not made any mention of such a party, but then the sergeant hadn't seemed overly trustful of Rhett, and could have deliberately held back information about one.

He studied the dust as it drew closer and decided whoever was kicking it up had spotted him and was making directly for him. He felt his dread begin to grow.

The false bottom of the wagon had been skillfully built by some Copperhead carpenter, using weathered lumber to blend with the original construction, a perfect match to the real bed. Still, he could never be sure the handiwork would not be detected by somebody with a suspicious eye.

He reached behind him and drew from a case a pair of army field glasses. He focused them on the approaching riders, struggling to hold them steady against the jostling of the wagon, finally halting the team.

He held the glasses for a long time, until he was sure. He lowered them then, shoved them back into the case, and swore. Indians, by God! Six of them. Cheyenne warriors by the looks of them.

He felt his spine prickle and cast an estimating glance at the weather-gashed terrain now visible ahead. If he could reach that, he might find some cover. Out here, in the open, the wagon itself would provide no protection against attack.

He wasn't sure which was the stronger, his relief that the riders weren't another bunch of bluebelly soldiers, or his fear that the Cheyennes were out to raise hell.

Even if their intentions weren't warlike to start, the sight of a lone white man with a team of mules that could be bartered to Santa Fe traders along the trail could change their mood quick enough. He knew Indians well enough to realize that.

Even if they were some of Black Kettle's truce-signing Arkansas River Cheyennes.

And if they were roving Cheyenne Dog Soldiers from up along the Platte, his chances could be less than slim.

He whipped the team, urging them on toward the only refuge in sight, the gashed area directly ahead. He took some comfort in his estimate that he was closer to his goal than the Cheyennes were to theirs. Not that they wouldn't follow. But if he could get in there deep enough to find cover—he snapped the lash above the mules again.

He reached and plunged recklessly into the sheltering terrain, and felt a momentary relief.

And at that moment the right rear wheel struck hard against a boulder and shattered.

The corner of the wagon dropped, the load of bullion shifted and smashed its way out of the false bed, spilling its glitter onto the ground.

The team came to a halt.

Rhett jumped down and rushed back to stand dismayed, staring at the sight, cursing his recklessness.

He remembered the Indians and went a few steps beyond until he could peer from concealment out onto the plain. He was surprised to see that they had come to a halt less than a mile away. And even as he watched, they wheeled about and went racing back the way they had come.

Then he saw the reason. Some four miles away, the patrol led by the sergeant who had accosted him earlier was jogging relentlessly toward him.

His mind raced. Why were they coming back? Whatever the reason, they would be quickly upon him. And there lay the load of gold bars glittering in the sun, waiting to betray him.

He ran toward it, stood for a moment desperately looking around for some way to hide it. If only he had the time, he could dig a hole and bury it, with the shovel he had in the wagon, and hope somehow to return later and recover it.

But by now the patrol was another mile closer and coming on fast.

A few feet away to the west, above the stranded wagon, an arroyo took a turn toward the south, leaving a sharp-rimmed cutbank where it curved.

Without another thought, he began grabbing up the bars

and running to the precipitous edge and throwing them into the arroyo. The bars were small but heavy, and he was soon sweating, partly from exertion, partly from fear he would run out of time.

At last he dropped the final one. He peered then over the edge, and they shone up at him, bright as ever.

He ran again to the wagon, tore free the shovel from a shifted mess of feed and miscellaneous junk. He returned, running, to the arroyo rim and, disregarding his own safety, began breaking away chunks of the precipice. In a matter of minutes he had started an avalanche of earth cascading down to cover the ingots. When he was certain they were hidden, he went back to the wagon, tossed the shovel into it, and hoped the dust rising from the arroyo bottom would settle quickly.

He was lucky; it did.

He was standing, staring at the broken wheel, when the patrol rode up.

"Busted down," the sergeant said. "A big, heavy wagon like this. Something fishy about this whole thing, reb. And that's why we turned back to follow you."

"Wheel hit that rock," Rhett said. "Did you see those Injuns off to the west? They had me hurrying."

"We saw them," the sergeant said. "But to me, it was you that seemed more interesting."

"In what way?"

"That I ain't sure of."

"Well, I'm damned glad to see you. Both on account of those Cheyenne, and account of this busted wheel."

"How do you know they were Cheyenne?"

"I got some field glasses."

"Even so. Ain't many except Injun-fighters can tell one kind of Injun from another."

"We had a few Cheyenne down Texas way, time to time," Rhett said.

"You ever fight any?"

"Time to time, yes."

"Then you been army."

"I told you," Rhett said, "I always been a civilian."

"How then?"

"I had a ranch once. I was raided a time or two."

"Why ain't you ranching now?"

"I got a touch of gold fever, I reckon. Like a million other fools. Heard about the rich strikes in Colorado and had to make my try. Sold my ranch and hoped to get lucky."

"And?"

"You see what I got left." Rhett gestured at the wreckage. "Looks like I traded a hardscrabble ranch for a team of mules and a busted wagon."

"I still think you got something of the army about you," the sergeant said. He was staring at the broken wagon bed. "Never saw a wagon bust like that."

"A freak accident, right enough," Rhett said. "I never saw anything quite like it myself."

The sergeant had ridden closer, and now he suddenly dismounted, stepped over to the wagon and felt it with his hand. "By God!" he said. "It's got a double bottom!"

Rhett pretended surprise. "What you reckon it was built that way for? To strengthen it for hauling ore samples?"

"I ought to be asking you," the sergeant said.

"Like I told you, I bought it from a miner up in the diggings. He never mentioned how it was built."

"Damned peculiar," the sergeant said. "Leastwise it looks so to me. But then, I ain't a freighter."

"Neither am I," Rhett said. "Not yet."

"If you intend to freight on the Santa Fe Trail, you better learn to handle a rig better than you do now."

Rhett showed him a grin. "I aim to learn."

The sergeant said, abruptly, "We'll take you into Fort Lyon with us. The wagon will have to stay. Might be you can hire somebody around the fort to come out and fix it. But we'll help you drive in the mules."

He still sounded suspicious, and Rhett felt it was no time to argue. What was there to argue about, anyway? The sergeant was right. There was no way to move the wagon, and he couldn't leave the mules to die or wander or be taken by the Cheyennes. He said, "I surely appreciate you doing that, suh."

The sergeant grunted, then said, "All right, get your team unhitched."

Later, mounted on one of the wheel mules, and taking with him only his revolver, carbine, a canteen, and the army field glasses, Rhett had a feeling he might not get back to the abandoned wagon—and the cache of gold—for a while. It didn't do much for his peace of mind.

At that moment, the sergeant spoke, and his words made Rhett's mood even worse. The sergeant said, "When we get to the fort, reb, you can expect to be interrogated."

CHAPTER 2

MAJOR Edward Warren, the current commanding officer at Fort Lyon, was a fair-minded man with ambivalent feelings about the Indians, particularly the Cheyennes. He did not share the "only good Indian is a dead Indian" opinion of his superior, Colorado Volunteers Colonel John M. Chivington.

He also abhorred the colonel's attitude regarding the killing of Indian children in enemy Cheyenne encampments, as expressed by Chivington so succinctly in "Nits make lice."

Still, he was a realistic officer who believed that force was a necessary evil to achieve the U.S. Government policy of Manifest Destiny that would settle the West.

He was a lean and tough man for his age, which was early forties, not wholly military in his bearing but competent in his command.

Now he sat at his desk, two armed troopers just outside his open door, confronting Rhett with a studied appraisal.

Rhett silently waited for him to speak.

When the words came, his tone was hard enough, but not accusing. "Sergeant Eilers has made a detailed report of his encounter with you yesterday. As you are aware, your mules are in our corral and being taken care of. I trust you've found our company mess palatable."

"Yes, suh. I'm greatly obliged."

"Had a near run-in with some Cheyennes, I understand."

"I did. Lucky for me your sergeant decided to return with his patrol about that time."

The major nodded. "Quite lucky, I'd say. However, his

12

return was based not upon his completion of his scout northward, but because your presence in the area continued to bother him."

Rhett hesitated, then said, "In what way, Major?"

The major shrugged. "We have learned to be suspicious of all southerners in the West. We are well aware that there are Copperheads, rebel sympathizers, throughout the territories."

"I am a Texan, Major."

"Still a southerner," Warren said. "Possibly less suspect than would be a Virginian or a Georgian, but still a southerner."

"I consider myself a westerner, suh."

"Yes. The sergeant mentioned that you claim some experience fighting Comanche and Kiowa. Even some knowledge of Cheyenne. That only serves to pique my suspicions."

"In what way, Major?"

"A southerner who also has familiarity with Indian ways could well be one of those insidious agents we know are working for the Confederacy to stir up the tribes here on the frontier. The idea being, of course, to force the Union to withdraw troops from the southern front to regarrison our abandoned posts out here with regulars."

"Sounds a mite farfetched a scheme," Rhett said.

"I differ there. We have reason to believe the recent resurgence of hostile attacks on whites by the tribes, after a period of considerable peace, is due directly to the work of Confederate agents working clandestinely among them. This is now a widespread opinion."

"And you think I may be one of these agents?"

Major Warren did not answer. Instead he simply kept a steady stare on Rhett's face.

Rhett did not flinch under the stare. He met the major's eyes and held them. "I would never stir up Injuns to kill whites, suh. I have seen the handiwork of Comanches on at least two ranch families in Texas. It is something I never want to see again."

The major was thoughtful, then said, "If you have seen Indian atrocities, what you say could well be true. I have seen some, and I can share your revulsion."

"It is something you can never forget," Rhett said.

"However, I feel I must keep you under detainment for now."

"Detainment? For how long, suh?"

"Until I have the opportunity to think about this, and to send a detachment back to where you wrecked the wagon. Sergeant Eilers was apparently negligent in his search of its contents. He could not be specific enough in describing them to my satisfaction. He could not be certain there were no trade goods involved, although you appeared to be carrying a light load for such a heavy wagon. Even a small amount of trade goods, particularly weapons, could buy Indian allies for the rebels."

"I am not fool enough to roam Cheyenne country alone with a wagonload of guns or ammo, Major."

"I would find that easier to believe," Major Warren said, "if we hadn't found you out there doing just that, with or without the trade goods." He paused. "We have found that the misdirected patriotism of Confederate sympathizers can lead them to take unbelievably foolish risks. And you strike me as the type of man who is not afraid of danger."

"I carried no trade goods," Rhett said. "Least of all, weapons."

The major had been staring at him all through their talk, and now, suddenly, a startled expression came to his face. He said, abruptly, as if he could not restrain the words, "Glorieta Pass!"

"Suh?"

"Glorieta Pass, by God! From the beginning I thought there was something familiar about you. You were with the

Texans left to guard Scurry's Confederate train of supply wagons at Johnson's Ranch behind the battle line."

"Why do you say that, suh?"

"Goddammit! I saw you. I was a lieutenant with Major Chivington's Colorado detachment when we went over the mountain trail south of the pass and caught you by surprise."

Rhett's thoughts went back to that day more than two years ago, late March of 1862. He'd been there, one of the walking wounded from the battle at the Apache Canyon entry to the pass two days before. Sent back to join a handful of other Texans detailed to guard the sixty-wagon train loaded with ammunition, clothing, commissary items, forage, and surgical supplies needed for the projected campaign to capture Fort Union and take New Mexico for the South.

They had been taken by surprise as Chivington's battalion came plunging down from the unknown mountain back-trail to overwhelm them and completely destroy the train, setting it afire.

Chivington's men had killed many and captured seventeen, including some officers. Rhett was one of them.

A rumor quickly spread that Chivington had given orders to shoot the seventeen if the Union men were attacked as they withdrew toward the Federal camp. True or not, it had driven Rhett to escape during the long night's march.

But not before he had given his name and rank to the Union officer now seated before him. Thinking back on it, he now cursed himself for doing so. He also cursed the major's astute memory—and his own lousy one, for until this moment he had not remembered their former meeting. He had been suffering from a reopened arm wound and exhaustion and had not been too clear in the head at that time, he supposed.

Now he said, "Near two and a half years ago, Major."

Warren frowned with his effort to remember. "Captain Justin Rhett, Texas Cavalry," he said.

"You have a good memory, suh."

"Then you do not deny it?"

"Would it do me any good?"

"None whatsoever. I remember you because, even though you were wounded, you were the only one of our prisoners who got away."

"And now?"

"What are you doing here?"

"I quit the war, Major, went back to my ranch, sold it and tried mining."

"And can you prove it?"

"Why else would I be here?"

"I mean, can you prove you quit the Confederate armed forces?"

"Am I wearing a uniform?"

"Means nothing," the major said. "Rhett, I'm going to have to hold you here on possible charges of spying."

"I am not a spy, suh."

"Perhaps. But under the circumstances, what would you do in my position?"

Rhett had no answer for that.

"I'd be a damned fool to let you go unless I have orders from the regiment commander to do so."

Rhett felt his hope sinking. "Chivington?" he said.

"*Colonel* Chivington, yes."

Rhett's hope hit bottom.

CHAPTER 3

THEY put him in the guardhouse.

Almost immediately he began thinking how he might escape. And knowing that escape was the nearest thing to impossible that he had ever faced. The holding cell was built of stone walls, with a mud-covered willow-poled flat roof. There was a hard-packed dirt floor. Besides which there was always an enlisted man on watch in the adjacent guardroom.

It was from one of the guards that Rhett learned what was going on while he was being held.

"Ain't no harm in telling you this, reb," the guard said. "Give you something to worry about, and that would please me no end. Teach you to stay down south where you belong, fighting like a man should, instead of stirring up these damned redskins and getting real soldiers like me killed by them."

"You won't find Texans collaborating with Injuns," Rhett said.

"You say. Well, Tex, I guess we may soon find out. The major done sent Sarge Eilers back to examine your busted wagon, and he give him instructions to go over it with a fine-toothed comb. Major done give him hell for not doing that when he run onto you. Old Sarge, he damned sure ain't going to miss any evidence you been carrying Injun trade rifles this time." The guard paused, as if relishing some thought. "Reb, mighty soon now you may be facing a firing squad. We ain't regular army here, and us Coloradans got our own ideas on how to handle the Injun problems."

Trade rifles, Rhett thought wryly. He wished that was all

17

he had to worry about. His great fear was that Sergeant Eilers would find the gold bars.

And if he did, Rhett would get the kind of interrogation that no man could hold out against. Greed for gold could change most any interrogator into a torturing savage.

And if he gave away the secret, he'd give away all chance of Old Pap Price saving the Confederacy on the western border. He, Rhett, would fail the South.

It had been a fool mission to send one man alone to bring a half million dollars in gold across two territories and a part of a state.

But there had been a lot of fool decisions made during this war, on both sides.

His chance came when they jailed the half-breed. The new prisoner was the son of a white trader and a Cheyenne mother, and he had been a sometime scout for the army, and more recently for the Colorado Volunteers. This much he revealed to Rhett after he had been thrust, drunk, into an adjacent cell by the corporal of the guard. The half-breed was young and light skinned, with only a slight Indian cast to his features.

"They arrested one of their own scouts?" Rhett asked. He was intrigued by the educated way the scout spoke.

"I got drunk and slapped around a Yankee sergeant."

"You speak of Yankees—"

"I was in the reb army for a while. My pa made good money trading, being married into the tribe, and he sent me to Saint Louis to a boarding school and later an academy. Most of my classmates were southern sympathizers and some left to join up with Price. So did I. I was in the Battle of Pea Ridge in Arkansas in 'sixty-two. Got a bellyful of white man's warfare there, and left like a lot of others.

"Deserted?"

"Call it that. More than a few did likewise. I came back and went to live with my mother's people for a while. Didn't take to that either. Ended up scouting, and trying to mediate between the Indians and the soldiers. Now I've got a stomach full of that too." He was beginning to sober up, and looked closely at Rhett. "Name of George Lawler. I heard about your case before I got in my own trouble this afternoon."

Rhett was silent, thinking.

Lawler said, "They claim you're a reb that fought against Major Warren at Glorieta Pass."

Rhett said, "You still like the South?"

"Some. But the South is beaten. You must know that."

"There's a lot of fight left in Price," Rhett said. "And I was headed back to rejoin him." He did not mention the gold.

"What're you doing in Colorado?"

"I can't tell you that."

"Stirring up Indians? Getting my mother's people killed?"

"I've had no part in any such plot."

Lawler was silent, then he said, "You know, the white man part of me has always felt guilty about deserting. How well do you know Price?"

Rhett shrugged. "I have a captain's rank. But I am personally acquainted."

"If I went back, you think I'd be accepted?"

"I could arrange that," Rhett said. He wasn't at all sure of this, but he was desperate.

"So you want to get out of here," Lawler said.

"Price is expecting me."

"You'll never make it. Not without help."

"Where will I get any?"

The educated half-breed appeared to make a decision. "Possibly from me."

"When will they let you out?"

"Any time now. With me it's happened before. Things build up inside me and I get drunk. I get a little wild and they throw me in here. Once the firewater is out of my blood, they let me out. They got a use for me, because of my ties to the Cheyenne.''

At nine o'clock of the second night following, just as the trumpeter was sounding tattoo, the yelling of a party of Cheyennes in the dark beyond the gate startled the fort.

The man on guard outside the cell block said, "Christ! What's going on? Them Injuns never make a ruckus after dark!'' He ran outside the guardhouse, leaving Rhett unwatched.

The other cells were empty. Lawler had been released the first morning, and Rhett knew now it had given the half-breed time to do what Rhett had asked. To round up some of his Cheyenne relatives to create a diversion.

Rhett had asked him to do that, after Lawler had told him there was a way out of the other cell. "I found it out by accident the last time they jailed me," Lawler said. "Some inmate had it almost made, but never got a chance to use it. I never have because I've never been held more than a few hours." He paused. "Only thing, you'd have to get into this cell to take advantage of it.''

"Maybe I can talk the sergeant of the guard into switching me, somehow," Rhett said.

"I'll come back after I'm released," Lawler said, "and see if you've made it.''

It had taken a mixture of persuasion and needling on Rhett's part to do it. First he had managed to loosen a bolt in the wall, which held his bunk suspended by a chain. This made the bunk temporarily unusable.

Even so, the guard acceded to Rhett's request for transfer only because he took a perverse pleasure in seeing the reb locked up in the cell which had just housed "that damned Injun-breed scout I never trusted. You that's been working with the red bastards, trying to stir them up against us, you want to sleep in his bunk, I'll let you. But you'll use his blankets. Maybe you'll catch Injun lice from them.''

Now, as the commotion outside the fort diverted the attention of all personnel, Rhett lay prone and reached under the bunk fastened to the outside wall and dug with his fingers into a spot in the earth floor that Lawler had loosened.

He uncovered and grasped the end of a wide, thin plank covered only by a couple of inches of packed dirt. Awkwardly, he struggled to lift it, and slowly swung it toward him, pivoting on the opposite end.

He found a hole excavated from beyond the wall. In the semidarkness of the cell, he groped until he was sure its depth cleared a shallow foundation, then slid into it on his back and wriggled his way out, pushing loose some dirt-covered boards outside.

Seconds later he was staring at stars, glimpsed through the branches of a cluster of screening brush.

A hand reached down to help him up, and the half-breed's voice said, "Make it fast!"

They raced away from the fort's wall. A few hundred yards away and in the shelter of a thin fringe of willows along the banks of the Arkansas River, a Cheyenne waited with horses.

Lawler said, "This is my cousin, Lone Buffalo. He is a Cheyenne Dog Soldier, and very brave."

The Cheyenne's face was hard to see in the dark, but Rhett judged he was a young, strong warrior. He said, in halting English, "I do this because my cousin ask. Not for a white man."

The half-breed said to Rhett, "You will remember Lone Buffalo, eh, Captain? If ever you meet again—"

"I will remember," Rhett said with feeling. "It will be a debt I owe." He held out his hand.

Lone Buffalo was slow to take it, and his grasp was not friendly. He said again, "I only do this because of my cousin," and withdrew his hand. He turned abruptly and leaped onto one of the Indian ponies, and rode off in the direction of the still-yelling Cheyennes on the other side of the fort, beyond the gate.

Lawler and Rhett mounted the other horses, and Rhett said, "Your cousin is not a friendly man."

"He hates whites. He only agreed to help when I told him you are a Confederate on the other side."

"I'm obliged to him for what he did," Rhett said. "And I'm obliged to you more than I can say."

Lawler held up his hand. "The noise has stopped. The Cheyenne are gone." He turned his mount toward the fort.

Rhett said, "You aren't coming?"

"I changed my mind. My people need me here. I can sometimes look out for their rights."

Rhett nodded. "I understand."

"There'll be a patrol on your trail in the morning," the half-breed said. "You'd better ride hard, Captain."

Rhett turned south and splashed across the river. He did not look back.

Two weeks later, Rhett reached central Arkansas, and found Price's army no longer encamped where he had left it. The restless general had decided his invasion could not wait. He had started north with an army of twelve thousand men, but only eight thousand of them were armed.

He hoped, apparently, to recover arms from the Union troops he expected to vanquish.

That was Old Pap Price, Rhett thought. The nickname came from his white hair, not from any lack of ebullience.

Rhett cursed the delays and troubles that had kept him from arriving in time, and, worse yet, from completing his mission to bring the needed gold for the underequipped troops.

Then, grimly, he rode to catch up with the invaders, his thought now to report to the general his failure, and to then rejoin his command to share whatever fate befell it.

As he neared the Confederate troops, his dismay grew at seeing the rags of uniforms many were clothed in.

But when, finally, he caught up with Price himself, as the army crossed the Arkansas River between Little Rock and Fort Smith, he learned, at least partly, why Price felt he could no longer wait.

Rumor had come that Union General Sherman was about to march through Georgia, laying waste the entire state, and Price hoped to divert this catastrophe from the southern heartland by his own bold action in the West.

Rhett's conversation with the general was disappointingly brief. Price was plainly preoccupied now by his drive on Missouri and his goal to take Kansas for the South.

With a promise to discuss the aborted mission in the future, Rhett found himself sent back to Brigadier General Marmaduke's cavalry. The company of Texans he had commanded was now led by another.

Through late September he fought with this unit, wearing the coat of a sergeant who had been killed in a first skirmish. The scarcity of clothing, and the cold of night, made such salvaging a common practice.

On September 26, Marmaduke's force reached the Union fort at Pilot Knob, and two days later it was in southern hands.

They next paused near Jefferson City, then bypassed it on a hunch of Price's and struck for Boonville, forty miles to the northeast.

The fall of Lexington followed, and then at Waverly they confronted the Union General Blunt and began a week-long running battle through a hundred and fifty miles of western Missouri, with Blunt's brigade constantly falling back.

Unknown to the Confederates, Wild Bill Hickock rode with Blunt, scouting for the Union forces, slipping back and forth through the lines with his information.

Despite this, they took Independence.

Then, on October 23, came the Battle of Westport, near Kansas City.

The Federals, suddenly reinforced by the troops of Generals Curtis and Pleasanton to a total of twenty thousand against Price's nine thousand active, soon had Old Pap retreating south.

Price's army marched through a long night, harried by Union pursuers, and at dawn he ordered Marmaduke to deploy on a prairie below the Marais des Cygnes River, as rear guard.

And there they were attacked by the pursuers in an epic melee of rival cavalry. The Federals charged in a column of regiments, bugles blowing, a whole brigade fighting on horse and afoot, and Marmaduke's men retreated. Marmaduke's horse threw him and he was captured.

The rest of Price's army made its way to eventual escape into the Indian Territory, but a long line of captured Marmaduke cavalrymen were herded into Fort Scott. They would soon enough be taken north to the prisoner-of-war pens for captured rebels.

Captain Justin Rhett, still wearing his salvaged Confederate jacket, with its sergeant's stripes, was among them.

February 1865, Rock Island, Illinois. United States prisoner-of-war camp for Confederate captives.

The camp commandant, in his colonel's uniform, sat behind his desk while the recruitment officer, a major sent from Washington, stood by waiting.

The door to the anteroom opened and an orderly spoke to the colonel. "Prisoner Justin Rhett is here, sir."

"Send him in," the commandant said.

The man in the tattered gray with a sergeant's stripes shuffled in. He stood just inside the door, emaciated and slouched, and stared from one Union officer to the other with hard, feverish eyes.

"Step forward and identify yourself," the commandant said irritably.

The prisoner stiffened at the tone, and his eyes fastened on the colonel's. There was a silent staring between them. Then, slowly, the prisoner moved forward and came rigidly to attention. He said, "Justin Rhett, Army of the Confederate States of America."

"Is that how you address an officer in the rebel army?"

"Army of the Confederate States of America, *suh!*"

"That's better," the commandant said. He turned to the major. "Go ahead, Major Ronstadt."

The major said, "Thank you, sir," and gave his attention to the man in gray. "What part of the South are you from, Rhett?"

"I am a Texan."

"You are a Texan, *what?*"

"I am a Texan, *suh!*"

"Get back in the habit of acting like a soldier," the major said.

"Sorry, suh. It has been a long time."

The major referred to a paper he held in his hand. "Since November of last year. A lot of months in this hell-hole."

"Yes, suh."

The commandant scowled at this description of his prison, but he said nothing.

The major went on, "You were taken captive as you fled after the Battle of Westport. One of Marmaduke's men. Is that correct?"

"No, suh. We were not fleeing. We were the rear guard for General Price's retreat. We fought a bitter cavalry set-to with Pleasanton's men and were finally overrun. My horse was shot from under me before I was taken."

The major nodded. "Your record shows that since you have been here you have continued to act in conformance with your sergeant's stripes in maintaining a modicum of discipline among the men around you. Had you been a sergeant long?"

"No, suh."

"You were not an experienced noncom?"

"I was a captain."

The commandant looked startled. The major did not.

After a brief silence, the major said, "You made no effort to identify yourself as an officer? Had you done so, you would have gone to an officer's prison."

"I tried to explain at first, suh. I was not believed. Before I could get someone to vouch for me, I was separated into a bunch being railroaded here. I had been on detached duty, and there had been many new replacements in the unit I was fighting with who did not know I previously held command. Wearing these stripes was foolish of me, maybe, but we were poorly equipped, and a man will wear anything when it's cold."

The major nodded. "The processing of captives can be a time of great confusion—slipups do occur."

Rhett gestured to the papers held by the officer. "It is my feeling, suh, that you are not entirely surprised by what I have just said."

The major did not answer. Instead, he said, "Possibly we could transfer you to a camp for officers. But the exchange of prisoners between North and South is no longer being done, due to War Department policy changes. You could be there a long wait."

"I would prefer that to here, suh."

"Would you prefer that to freedom?"

"Freedom, suh?"

The major said, "I have requested your being brought in here because, as you have undoubtedly heard, we are recruiting Confederate prisoners to go west and garrison the frontier forts which the exigencies of the war have forced us to abandon."

"Yes, suh. I have heard some talk about it."

"Would you prefer fighting Indians to continued imprisonment?"

Rhett stared hard at the commandant, seated listening to all of this. "Yes, suh," he said. "I would prefer fighting Injuns to staying here in this pigpen you call a prison."

As Rhett was led away in custody of a guard, the Union officers faced each other.

The commandant said, "You want him for the regiment of Galvanized Yankees I've been requested to let you organize here?"

"Yes, sir. However, I'm requesting he be given a sergeant's rank and the command of a detachment with a measure of autonomy. We have a special mission for former Captain Justin Rhett of the Army of the Confederacy."

The colonel gave the major a cynical appraisal. "I see. It seems to me that you were already well aware of his background before you questioned him."

The major smiled faintly. "We have spent some time tracing him down. While doing so we have learned some interesting facts about him. Facts that I am under special orders not to reveal."

The commandant thought about this for a long moment. Then he said, "Tell me this, Major. When he has done what you want him to do . . . ?"

The major said, "He's a rebel officer, isn't he? As such he's easily expendable." He paused. "And now, if I may have the use of your office privately for a few minutes, Colonel?"

The commandant frowned. "I do not like this cloak-and-dagger stuff, Major."

Ronstadt seemed unperturbed. "You have seen my credentials, Colonel. And the Secret Service's request for your complete cooperation."

"Bring your spy out," the commandant said. "Is there any reason I can't be present?"

Major Ronstadt hesitated. "Well, I suppose not, sir." He

turned toward a partly closed closet door and raised his voice slightly. "All right, Fenton, come out."

The tall, rugged-looking man in civilian clothes stepped forth. He had an outdoor look about him, and his age was hard to judge.

"You heard the conversation," Major Ronstadt said. "Did you get a good look at him?"

"That I did, sir," Fenton said.

CHAPTER 4

THE U.S. Volunteer Regiment, somewhat contemptuously called the Galvanized Yankees, of which Justin Rhett was now a sergeant, was immediately railed to Fort Leavenworth.

There, wearing the hated blue uniform, they spent a few weeks drilling while they awaited orders that would send them west.

The orders came, and most slogged their way three hundred fifty miles through a slowly thawing winter to Fort Kearny.

They were now in the Department of the Plains, based in Denver, Colorado, and commanded by a veteran frontier general, Patrick Connor. From his base, Connor telegraphed his orders for the disposition of the regiment. "Two companies at each of Kearny, Cottonwood, Julesburg, Junction, and Laramie. Headquarters of regiment will be at Julesburg."

He then divided the regiment further "in small parties of one noncommissioned officer and twelve privates each stationed at various points generally ten miles apart on the line of the Overland Mail route for the purpose of guarding citizens and their property from attacks of hostile Indians."

Ben Holladay of the Overland Stage and Mail had demanded military guards and escorts. The U.S. Government, desperate to keep transcontinental travel and mail delivery functioning, was giving him what he wanted.

The regiment was spread out over six hundred miles of frontier road, along which were established stage stations every ten to twelve miles.

Some stage stations had been established at road ranches,

29

former crude taverns that had been serving earlier travelers along the trails for years. They were often no more than sod walls, brush-and-mud-covered roofs, and tamped-earth floors.

A main house would contain a living room, storeroom, and a room or two for overnight guests. Food and drink were sold and served in the storeroom. Around the main structure were the stables and corrals where riding stock and relief teams for the stagecoaches were kept.

The Overland stage stops were mostly swing stations, where teams were merely changed. But every fifth or sixth was a home station, which put up blacksmiths, carpenters, stock tenders, harness repairmen, and stage drivers.

These larger stations frequently drew other businesses, saloons, mercantiles, and dancehalls, and sometimes a small town would grow from one.

Such a one was Cheyenne Springs Station.

It was not, however, on the Holladay Stage Line, which ran generally along the Platte. It was, rather, on the old Smoky Hill River Trail to Denver, and was only now being used experimentally in a new attempt to compete against Holladay with a shorter route. Earlier attempts had failed, due to shifting economies of the Colorado capital.

That and the fact that the trail ran through the heart of the Cheyenne buffalo-hunting grounds north of the Arkansas.

It was a perplexed Sergeant Justin Rhett who watched the other units of the regiment leave for posts along the Platte, and then was inexplicably handed orders to take his own men to Cheyenne Springs, the length of Kansas away, and only sixty-odd miles northeast of Fort Lyon.

He could only assume that other detachments would be sent to the same route, but up to the time of his leaving Leavenworth this had not occurred. He was curious at first, but attributed his orders eventually to sheer good luck.

He had a great and urgent interest in a certain cache of gold bars somewhere in that area, and in its possible fate.

There had been some sporadic raiding along the Smoky Hill route during the summer of 1864, but the town of Cheyenne Springs had been spared.

The important truce-favoring Chief Black Kettle and his band of southern Cheyenne had been trying to live peacefully and had by example and persuasion brought other Cheyennes to their way of thinking.

And then, at the end of November, the bloodthirsty fool Colonel Chivington led a new troop of hundred-day enlistees, the 3rd Colorado Volunteer regiment, to look for Indians he could kill.

He found no hostiles and, bitterly frustrated, descended on Black Kettle's band in their winter camp on Sand Creek, northeast of Fort Lyon.

He attacked at dawn with over seven hundred troops and slaughtered 163 unsuspecting and innocent Indians, 108 of whom were women and children. His men, drunk on whiskey and bloodlust, and with his approval, scalped and mutilated most of them and even sliced off the breasts of slain squaws for trophies.

This, to become known as the Sand Creek Massacre, would arouse horror throughout the United States.

It would also enrage the Cheyenne and other Indians throughout the West, and unite them in a major effort to drive out the treacherous whites by wreaking vengeance.

As spring came to the plains, the attacks began.

And the people of Cheyenne Springs, like others elsewhere, waited in dread.

"One of these times," Doc Samuel Craig, the town's medico had been saying lately, "one of these times it will be our turn."

Jed Evans, who ran the mercantile, said, "When are they going to send us soldiers? Goddammit! Don't anybody back at Leavenworth hear us asking?" He was standing morosely beside Craig under the portico of his store.

Doc shook his head. "It isn't that, Jed. It's just that they've got nobody to send. Too many of our boys, like my son-in-law, have been chewed up and spit out by the war."

"One of these days it'll be us that gets chewed up—by the Injuns."

"We've been lucky so far," Craig said.

"Luck scares me," the storekeeper replied. "Those that live by luck die by it."

Sherry came out of the store just then, and Doc turned to study his daughter's face, to see if she had caught the conversation. He was eased when he read in her expression that she had not.

She was a pretty girl, but seldom smiling. Now she carried a box of groceries, and Evans said, "Did Junior get you what you wanted?"

Sherry nodded.

She was more than pretty, the storekeeper thought. She was beautiful. But the sadness that tinged her beauty was a thing you hated to see. Doc was a fool to keep her out here in this godforsaken trail town, just because he felt obligated to serve the locals.

If I was twenty-five years younger . . . , Evans thought. It was too bad about Sherry. Only nineteen. And already a widow.

The detachment, twelve men led by a sergeant, in trail-grimed but new-looking army blue, rode into the town.

"By God!" Jed Evans exclaimed. He had rushed outside his store as a townsman called in the door to alert him of the strange arrival. "By God! Our squawking has finally been answered!"

"Appears to be," the townsman said. "Ain't many, and them uniforms under that dust appear like they been recent recruited."

Evans was silent, studying the approaching horsemen. He said, "They don't ride like recruits. They ride like cavalry.

But the sergeant's stripes are white, not yellow. White is infantry."

"Simple," the townsman said. "They must be mounted infantry."

Evans scowled. "Hell, I ain't blind."

Sherry came out of her father's office and crossed the street to join them.

"Where's Doc?" the townsman said.

"Out on a call."

Evans said, "We got us some soldiers, Sherry."

She stood staring at the uniformed men, saying nothing.

The storekeeper glanced at her and thought, She can't forget her husband.

The troopers rode close and the sergeant halted his horse in front of them. He did not dismount. He looked at the townsmen without smiling, then his eyes went to the girl and he tipped his campaign hat.

"Welcome, Sergeant," Evans said. "Believe me when I say we're glad to see you." He stepped close to the mounted man and held up his hand.

There was a brief hesitation before the man in uniform took it. He still did not smile. "Rhett," he said. "Sergeant Rhett, suh. First squad, Company I, Third Regiment of U.S. Volunteer Infantry."

"U.S. Volunteer Infantry?"

For the first time the sergeant smiled, a faint and bitter smile. "Surely, suh, you have heard of us by now."

Evans looked at Sherry and saw no reaction on her face. He turned back to Rhett. "Yes, Sergeant. Of course. You've come to garrison the town, I presume."

"That we have, suh."

Sherry suddenly spoke. "You are from the South, Sergeant?"

A quick flush showed beneath Rhett's tan, but his face showed no expression. "Yes, ma'am. I judge you can tell that from my accent. I'm originally from Texas."

"Texas?" Her eyes flicked over his uniform. "How is it that you are wearing the uniform of the North?"

"As I said, ma'am, I am with a U.S. Volunteer Regiment. Perhaps you know us by a more derogatory term—Galvanized Yankees."

"I am not familiar with the term," Sherry said. "But if you are infantry, why is it you are riding?"

"It appears, ma'am, that those in high command have realized we need horses if we are to keep the stage roads free of Indians."

"Are all your men southerners?"

"Yes, ma'am."

She turned to Evans. "I don't think I understand."

Evans said, "These men have pledged themselves to come out here to protect us from the Injuns." He paused. "They are former Confederate captives." He faced her squarely as he spoke, always curious about her feelings. Always fantasizing, too, that perhaps he wasn't too old.

She turned from him then and addressed Rhett again. "My husband was killed last year," she said slowly. "He was with the Second Colorado, fighting to keep a Confederate force led by General Price from taking Kansas from the Union. Have you ever heard of that action, Sergeant?"

"Yes, I have, ma'am. And I'm very sorry about your husband—for your sake."

"And for his sake?"

A trace of anger flickered across his features and was gone.

"He was a soldier, ma'am, was he not?"

"Of course he was."

"Well, then."

"I see, Sergeant."

"I hope you do, ma'am. These are bad times for all of us. We can only hope that soon it will all be over."

She met his eyes and stared into them. "For me, Sergeant, it will never be over."

"I am sorry to hear that, ma'am," Rhett said again. Abruptly, he pivoted his mount and led his squad back toward the edge of the town where the stage station was. His orders were to bivouac there.

The Cheyenne Springs Station was a relic of an earlier attempt to establish a stage route, one of several that had failed. Now it had been resurrected to an extent, although basically it had been well designed for its purpose by its original builders.

The main building was rectangular, without offsets, and with slitted windows in all four mudbrick walls. When it was constructed, there had been no adjacent town, and its first owners had obviously been thinking of Indian attacks.

The spring, from which the town and station got its name, still flowed at the rear of the structure.

Off to the east side was the barn, with hayloft, but built of wood. Adjacent to it was a corral for the stage stock.

Except for a cluster of poplars near the spring, the compound was as bare as the surrounding country, more so even because any vestige of graze was quickly cropped by feeding animals.

There was also, beyond the barn, a slew of wooden outbuildings that comprised the workshops and the sleeping quarters for station personnel. Here lived and worked a pair of hostlers, a farrier, and a carpenter-handyman. Here, too, were overnight accommodations for the company stage drivers.

At the rear of the compound, beyond the spring, Rhett and his detachment set up their pup tents to make their bivouac.

The station keeper, Searle, and his wife, Esther, lived in the main building, and Esther cooked for all station hands as well as passengers.

It was a chore that was quickly draining away her earlier

comeliness; for the past four years of her marriage to Searle, she'd done this drudgery at several stations.

Searle himself was glumly taciturn, a strong but feeling young man saddened by the toll this life had taken on Esther. They were both still in their twenties, but she had aged faster, and for this he blamed himself. But he could see no way out. He had no other skills, and he could resign himself except when he looked at her.

If he could only get a decent stake some way, he thought, he would make a better life for her, and he would salvage what remained of the prettiness she'd had as his bride.

He had greeted the detachment, giving Rhett a handshake that was firm enough, if not warm. "Glad to have you," he said. "Although I been hoping they'd send us regular army for escorts."

Rhett was still considerably piqued by the reception given him in town by the girl. He said, "We are not green recruits, suh."

Searle showed nothing in his face, but he said quickly, "No offense meant, Sergeant."

Rhett guessed that he was aware of the detachment's background. And that he was glad enough to see it, even if he had let a glimpse of his prejudice show. Rhett said, "We are bluebellies now."

The station keeper nodded. "I saw you ride past a while ago, and I figured you weren't the ones I been expecting."

"I wanted to feel the town out a bit."

"Well, it's a Yankee-sympathizing town, as you might have expected."

"I somehow got that impression."

"I reckon the army'll be sending supplies along for you," Searle said. "And you'll have to take care of your own needs. I'm sorry, but my wife can't take on any more work, any more cooking than she now does."

"Of course. We're used to soldiers' mess. We'll be getting

spare horses, though, and they'll have to share your facilities."

"I'd guess the company knows that. They'll be glad to have you here."

"Kind of surprised at my orders myself," Rhett said. "Most of the regiment was sent out along Ben Holladay's line on the Platte."

"I guess the army moves in strange ways, though I never been a soldier."

"I have, and you're right," Rhett said.

"Was your own army the same?"

Rhett let him wait for an answer. Then he pinched the blue sleeve of his blouse and held it. "See this? This is my army now, mister."

"No offense meant," Searle said again. Then, defensively, "But you got to admit, this takes some getting used to."

"I wouldn't argue that," Rhett said.

Once they had their bivouac set up, the other noncom, Corporal Hall, came up to Rhett and stood beside him.

"You think it's going to work out for us, Cap'n?"

"Why not?"

"Yankee town, ain't it?"

"What else? We're in the North."

"Hard-nosed Yankees," the corporal said. "That girl in town, she strikes me as particular so."

"We killed her husband," Rhett said shortly.

"What you think the rest will be like?"

Rhett shrugged. "We got one thing going for us. They've been wanting soldiers out here bad." He paused. "They're Injun-scared, I reckon."

The corporal frowned. He was a small wiry man with dark tanned skin, black hair and wide mustache, and a hard, lined face that looked older than his body. He said, "Goddammit! Cap'n, don't let's linger too long. I got no wish to lose my scalp defending a bunch of damn Yankees."

Rhett was silent.

"You listening to me, Cap'n? The idea was to desert and get on with our business, soon as we got posted."

"In due time," Rhett said.

"How long?"

"We got to wait our chance. Don't forget they've got other troops posted. They could send them out after us."

"Hell, they'd be goddam Galvanized Yankees just like us. You think they'd bring us in?"

"There's gold involved here," Rhett said. "Where there's gold, you can't trust anybody."

"You're trusting us."

"I picked each one of you men for a reason," Rhett said. "That recruiting officer let me do it, and damned if I know why. But I picked you because I was sure you were still dedicated to the cause." He paused. "I didn't pick those they might send after us."

"How much time have we got?"

"Last I heard, General Jo Shelby was still in Texas. Only general that was refusing to surrender."

"You got a lot of admiration for him, ain't you?"

"I've seen him in battle. Him and his Iron Brigade," Rhett said. "And he saved Price's retreat. He took over the rearguard action after Marmaduke and us got taken."

"Is General Price going to Mexico with him?"

"I don't know. But Shelby damned sure is. He'll form a base there and harass the Union till they come to honorable terms for the South." Rhett paused. "That's all we can hope for now that Lee has surrendered. Honorable terms that will let the South return to how it was. Without the slaves, of course."

"You're dead set on taking that gold to Shelby, ain't you, Cap'n?"

"It was a mission I was given," Rhett said slowly, "to save the South. I failed. Now Shelby has given me a second chance."

"Hell, Shelby don't know nothing about that gold."

"I do," Rhett said. "And I know what it was destined for. I still aim to see it gets there." He paused again. "I picked you men because I thought each of you shared my feeling."

Corporal Hall said quickly, "We do, Cap'n. We surely do. And I reckon we all would be glad to fight for Shelby, too, from Mexico. It's just that we ain't wanting to risk our necks fighting for a bunch of damned northerners."

"We'll make our move at the first opportunity," Rhett said.

"It had better be soon, suh," the corporal said. "The men are getting impatient."

A westbound stage pulled into the station on the day following the arrival of Rhett's detachment. From among the passengers stepped a tall, well-built man in rumpled town clothes. The clothes did not seem to quite match the tanned, leathery look of his not unhandsome features.

Rhett, whose orders called for him to begin mounting his guard details on the morrow, had come forward from his tent quarters to witness the stage arrival. He was immediately struck by this contrast in the man's appearance. Instinctively, he moved forward to engage the man in conversation. "Rough trip, suh?"

The passenger looked at him, then grinned. "I'm used to rough trips, Sergeant. Just so long as you boys keep the Injuns off us, I always find the travel tolerable."

"We aim to do our best, suh," Rhett said.

"Can't nobody do more than that," the passenger said. "Well, I'll catch a meal here. I been told the lady here does the cooking provides a good one, all things considered."

"Going on, suh?"

The tall man kept his smile. "No. Got some business in town that may keep me a few days." He turned to pick up a worn valise as the swamper tossed it down from the stage boot. "Be staying at the hotel, if the town's got one." He looked down the dusty length of the main street until his eyes picked out the sign on the clapboard, two-story Smoky Hill Trail House.

"Enjoy your meal, suh," Rhett said.

"I near always do," the stranger said, and walked into the station, carrying his bag.

Rhett's glance went to the other passengers, but his mind returned to the one he had addressed. Rancher, he was thinking, or maybe a teamster. Even a frontier scout. Whatever he was, he didn't fit that suit of clothes too well.

The detachment settled down to the first week's routine of escorting the stages.

Rhett split his men into four details of three each, while he remained at the station to coordinate their movements.

This would also give him some time to work out the details of the plan that was his real purpose in coming west.

The guard run each way was about thirty-six miles. Then the details stayed over and returned with the next stage bound in the opposite direction.

It seemed like remarkably easy duty when Rhett thought about it. A little too easy, maybe.

He mentioned this to Searle, and the station keeper agreed. "But you got to remember, Sergeant, that if the line gets enough travel, they'll soon be running more stages."

"Yeah," Rhett said. But he still wondered.

His wonder increased when his first details reported back.

"Hell," Corporal Hall said. "We're the only Galvanized rebs on this route, I think. The guards that take over from us are Colorado bluebellies."

The returning guards from the opposite run told him the same.

Something wasn't right here, Rhett thought. He didn't like it.

CHAPTER 5

LEAVING the Smoky Hill Trail House, where he had taken a room, the tanned stranger in the town clothes made several inquiries about town, then paid a visit to Doc Craig's medical office.

He had picked a time after he had seen the doctor drive away in his buggy, apparently on a call, and he found Sherry alone cleaning out the quarters.

He was unknown to her, and she appraised him as a probable patient. "Doctor isn't in, sir."

"Wasn't the doctor I came to see, ma'am."

"Oh?"

"Name of Fenton, ma'am." He smiled. "And you are Sherry Cowper?"

"Yes."

He took an official-looking sheet of paper from an inner pocket of his coat, glanced at it once, then said, "Widow of Lieutenant Lyle Cowper, Second Regiment of Colorado Volunteer Cavalry, killed in action October twenty-third, eighteen sixty-four, at the battle of Westport, Missouri."

He kept his eyes on her as he spoke, and he saw the tears begin to form. He said, "My intentions were not to hurt you, ma'am. Still, the reawakening of your grief is proof that you may be able to serve the interests of your country."

"My country, Mr. Fenton? I do not understand."

"I am sure your loyalty to the Union has been only strengthened by the loss of your husband."

"Has not Lee surrendered?"

"Lee has. Not all other secesh generals have. There are

41

still diehards among them, along with many of lesser rank who wish to continue their misguided fight."

"And you, Mr. Fenton, what part do you have in this?"

He hesitated, then said, "I work for the government, Mrs. Cowper. In a branch whose intention is to stamp out these smoldering flames of rebellion as soon as possible, before they cost the lives of any more of our brave men. The South was wrong in rebelling, do you not agree?"

"Of course. And my husband would be alive today, if . . . if they hadn't."

"Exactly. And these diehards among them, intending to carry on with their fanaticism, can only bring more heartache to the womenfolk of the North. More widows like yourself, ma'am. Think of that. What would you do to stop that?"

In a burst of passion, she said, "Anything!"

"Then you may be of service to the Union."

"In what way?"

"There is a Galvanized Yankee sergeant in command of a detachment at the stage station. We suspect him of treason."

"Treason!"

Fenton nodded. "You have met him, I've heard. It is why I sought you out. You could be of great service to us if you were to cultivate a friendship with him."

"A friendship, Mr. Fenton?"

He nodded again. "A close friendship, Mrs. Cowper."

"I'm afraid that's impossible. I simply could not become friends with a Confederate soldier. I'm sure you can understand my feeling."

"You would be serving the memory of your husband," Fenton said. "Did you know that the sergeant was with Price at Westport? Think, ma'am, it was one like him who killed Lieutenant Cowper, possibly even he himself."

She looked shocked, then said, "But I fail to see how a spurious friendship with a rebel sergeant could serve the Union."

"A man out here, particularly a soldier, can get mighty lonely for a woman to confide in, ma'am. He could possibly reveal bits of information to you that could well help our cause."

"But I understand he has now taken an oath to serve our government—against the Indians."

"Against the Indians, Mrs. Cowper, yes. Perhaps, perhaps not. But would you trust his oath not to serve the South? Think of it. Think how strongly your own feeling is for the North, and you will realize how hard it is to trust the intentions of a dedicated rebel."

She was silently thoughtful for a long time. Fenton did not press her.

Finally, she said, "I will have to think of this, Mr. Fenton. It is not something on which one makes a snap decision."

"Certainly," Fenton said. "And when you reach your decision, ma'am, I will be at the Trail House."

The following day the Indians struck the station.

The eastbound stage from Denver came tearing down the road with Corporal Hall and Privates Howard and McGregor racing behind, turning occasionally to fire blindly into the dust cloud that partly obscured a dozen pursuing Cheyennes.

The stage careened into the foreyard. Zack Handy, the driver, hauled it to a stop and leaped down, a rifle in his hand. Ed Scofield, the shotgun guard, was a jump ahead of him, and turned to face the attackers riding into the yard, even as the mounted soldiers did likewise.

Zack ran around the stage and jerked open the door. He said, "Get out and get into the station!"

A woman, followed by two men, came bursting forth. They ran for the main house, Zack and Scofield now a step behind them.

The corporal and the privates fired into the dust, and drew an answering scatter of shots. They wheeled then and rode around the station, dismounted, dropped reins, and rushed into the building by the rear door.

Rhett, armed, came running in from the bivouac area and followed them in. Behind him came the six men on layover shift, carrying their weapons.

They all rushed into the front room. Esther left her kitchen to join them. Searle, who had started out to greet the arriving coach, only to be stopped in his tracks by the rushing passengers, was listening as Zack spewed out information.

"Dozen of the bastards," Zack was saying. "Started chasing us four, five miles back."

"Cheyenne?" Searle said.

Rhett was looking out through a window slit. He thrust his Spencer carbine through the opening and fired, even as a barrage from the attackers slammed against the heavy walls of the station.

"What else?" Zack said.

The troopers now had positions at the openings, shoving aside the men passengers who had been looking out.

There was no yip-yelling from the Cheyennes.

Zack said, "The bastards don't want to rouse the town, likely."

The shotgun, Scofield, said, "You damn fool, the shots'll rouse them."

Searle said, "It'll be the horses they're after."

As he said it, the Cheyennes turned away from their brief barrage and raced toward the corral and the stables.

Rhett saw this and rushed for the rear door. "Some of you men take the east windows," he called. "Hall, you come with me."

"I knew we'd ought to got on with our business," the corporal muttered as he caught up with him.

"I'll decide," Rhett said.

"Yes, *suh!*" Hall said.

Shots came from an outbuilding, and a Cheyenne fell off his horse just as he reached the corral gate.

A puff of smoke came from the blacksmith shop.

"Damned farrier is a good shot," Hall said.

There was a stack of cordwood close to the door, and they dropped behind it and began firing at the huddled Cheyennes trying to reach the corral.

Two of them got to the gate together and swung it open, and with excited yells now, the others rode around the outside to spook the corralled horses.

The horses rushed toward the opened gate as the Cheyennes wheeled again and raced forward to flank them.

"Now!" Rhett yelled, and he and Hall and the others inside at the windows opened up with their carbines.

The Cheyennes went down all over the place, as if a huge scythe had cut them off at seat height.

"Wild and crazy," Corporal Hall said. "They got no sense at all."

"They didn't figure on soldiers forted up here," Rhett said, working the triggerguard-lever that thrust another cartridge into his Spencer's breech. He fired and missed as a screaming young brave ducked low and rode straight toward the wood stack.

Hall shot him off his horse, but the frenzied Indian pony kept coming, smashed chest-on against the cordwood and sent it flying. The impact bowled both men over.

The other Cheyennes split around the station and kept going, riding off into the prairie. The men inside the building fired scattered shots from the west window slits as they reached them, but they were too late to be effective.

Six Cheyennes lay around the corral, besides the one near the woodpile. That one looked dead, Rhett thought, and so did the rest of them. But he had seen enough wounded men play dead on the battlefields to be leery.

"We taking prisoners if they ain't dead?" the corporal said.

Rhett hesitated. But Zack and Scofield came out of the door in time to hear the question.

"Prisoners, hell!" Zack said. "You boys ain't fought many

Injuns, I reckon." He moved out cautiously with his rifle, saying, "Come along, Ed, here's where you can use that shotgun." Scofield followed.

At that moment the Indian nearest them moved slightly. Scofield blew his head off from six feet away.

"Christ!" the corporal said.

The troopers were outside too now, and Zack said, "Watch them dead corpses, boys. Even a dead Injun ain't always a good one."

They approached the scattered bodies, tense and alert. But only one other moved. One near the corral was lying prone, and dragged a rifle to firing position.

Rhett, almost too late, saw it and put another bullet into him.

"You had some experience with the bastards, I guess," Zack said. "Or did you treat our boys that way down south?"

Rhett did not answer him.

They went on scrutinizing the corpses. Zack said, "I reckon I hadn't ought to said that."

Rhett held his silence.

"Was these Dog Soldiers, we'd had a worse time," the driver said. "The Dog Soldiers are the top warrior society of the Cheyenne."

"How do you know they weren't?"

"Can't tell for sure, because they wasn't wearing war bonnets. A Cheyenne Dog Soldier, he don't have no tail feathers hanging down his back from his war bonnet. These wasn't wearing no feathers at all. Not on the warpath. Just a bunch of young bucks that attacked my stage on impulse."

Rhett said to Hall, "Get some men out rounding up those horses."

"Sure, Cap'n," Hall said. "But we got some wounded."

"Where?"

One of the troopers said, "Inside, Sarge. McGregor got it bad in the shoulder. Stuart's hit in the arm."

Rhett turned toward the station.

Searle came out and said, "We got to get those bodies buried."

Rhett passed by him without a word, concerned now about his men. Inside, Private Stuart was holding one of Esther Searle's towels against a flesh wound in his forearm.

"Damned Injun put one through the window, first thing," he said. "One got Mac there worse than me."

McGregor was sitting slumped against a wall with Esther bending over him, trying to stanch a flow of blood under his shoulder with her apron. His face was pale.

Esther looked up and said, "He's hurt bad, Sergeant. You'd best send somebody for Doctor Craig."

"Doctor Craig?"

"Down the road, middle of town," Esther said.

Rhett said to Stuart, "Get a man in here." He crouched down and removed Esther's hand holding the cloth from the wound. Blood welled from it.

Private Brogden came in. "Sarge?"

"Go down the street into town. There's a doctor got his office there. Bring him back on the double."

Brogden stared at the wounded man. "He don't look too good, Sarge."

"Get going!" Rhett snapped.

The trooper left hurriedly.

"We'd best lay him down, ma'am," Rhett said. "Can you get something to rest his head on?"

She undid her apron ties so he could hold the compress, and moved quickly toward the Searles' sleeping quarters. She was back in a moment with a pillow.

"I hope Doctor Craig is in," she said. "He takes care of everybody for miles around."

"You got settlers around here, ma'am?"

"Some. A few trying to farm. Desperate people, else why would they risk their lives with the Indians aroused? Most were there, though, before Chivington's massacre. But even so . . . "

"I've seen it happen down Texas way," Rhett said. "Against Comanches. People will take some terrible risks to make a living."

She said sadly, "Yes, Sergeant. We all do what we have to do."

Searle came in. "I got a couple of my men digging a hole to bury the Injuns, Sergeant. Your men are rounding up the stock."

"We going to lose any?"

"Don't think so. The beating those bucks took, they didn't fool with horses when they rode off. They scattered some, but a horse don't like to leave home no more than anybody else." He looked at McGregor. "We better get the doctor for him."

"Been sent for," Rhett said.

"First time we been attacked," Searle said. "I'm damn sure glad you were here, reb."

"Reb, eh?"

"Sorry. Like I said, it takes some getting used to."

The front door opened and Private Brogden stepped in. Behind him was Sherry Cowper, and beyond her Rhett could glimpse other people from the town.

Brogden said, "I met half the town rushing here on account the shooting, Sarge. The doc's gone to deliver a baby somewheres, but this here lady is his daughter and knows some medicine, she says."

Sherry pushed by him and went to the wounded man.

Rhett said, "Ma'am, are you a doctor?"

"No. But I have often helped my father."

Rhett said to Searle, "Keep the rest of that crowd out of here."

Searle went to the door and closed and bolted it.

Sherry was examining the wound. She said, "Have you looked at this, Sergeant?"

"Yes, ma'am."

"Then you saw there is no exit hole."

"Yes. The Injuns were firing old smoothbore weapons by the looks of them. Then, too, maybe the bullet ricocheted off that adobe windowsill and lost more velocity. A real freak shot, ma'am."

"The lead is still in him. And my father may be gone for hours. The settler's wife he's attending has a history of long hard labors."

"Is it safe to wait?"

"I don't know. The longer the wait, the greater the chance of infection. Once infected, the greater the . . . danger."

"Could you take it out?"

"I have assisted in such procedures. It is your decision, Sergeant."

"Do you have something to kill the pain?"

"Yes. At the office. I'd have to get what I need."

"Go ahead," Rhett said. "Please, ma'am."

She returned in a quarter hour, Brogden again accompanying her. Together they carried a small bag of instruments and a flask of chloroform.

The three passengers who had come in on the wild-riding stage were only just recovering from their experience, followed by the station attack, and were now faced with witnessing a surgical procedure. All three were Denverites, and knew each other. The two men were apparently merchants, and the woman was the daughter of the older man.

"No lack of excitement this trip," the younger man said to nobody in particular.

"Where are you bound?" Searle asked, although his interest was on Sherry's preparations, not on the young man's question.

"Kansas City, for a vacation."

"You're off to a bad start."

"That cussed Chivington sure stirred up a nest of rattlers," the older man said. "Ought to stood a court-martial for what he did at Sand Creek."

The younger man said, "He took the easy way out. Resigned from the service when he saw it coming."

"And left us to suffer for it," muttered the woman.

Sherry said, "I'll need a room apart to work on this."

"There's a guest room not used," offered Esther, and led the way to one of them.

"You can help, Sergeant," Sherry said. "The private, too, and Mr. Searle. Esther, I'll need hot water."

The men got McGregor on his feet and helped him into the room and onto a cot.

"Not much light from these slitted windows," Sherry said. "Somebody please get a couple of lamps and put them close by." She hesitated. "I've got chloroform, but there's always a risk in using it. Can you tolerate pain, soldier?"

"I reckon I could, ma'am, if there's some whiskey available."

Searle went out to the bar and came back with a bottle. He looked at Sherry, and she nodded, and he raised the private up and tilted the bottle so he could drink.

She waited until the liquor took effect, then said, "You men hold him steady." She took up a probe from her opened kit of surgical instruments.

Minutes passed, and McGregor tried to squirm, and groaned from behind clenched teeth, as Rhett and Brogden held him down.

Then, finally, she withdrew with her forceps a misshapen bullet, and threw it into a pan Esther had brought.

McGregor began to mumble, and cursed as she cleaned the wound with carbolic acid.

Rhett studied her and saw the thin film of sweat that covered her face. There was a beauty there, he thought, that no amount of sweat could tarnish. A beauty and a strength.

Looking at her caused his pulse to quicken. He turned away and focused on the patient. It did him no good to look at her. Not the way she felt about Confederates.

CHAPTER 6

RHETT thought about the Colorado Volunteer bluebellies that boxed him in at both ends of his escort run, and was aware that if his plans ever resulted in a showdown in the area, he would be outnumbered at least two to one.

His suspicions were aroused so strongly that he was afraid to make a move toward joining General Shelby. He decided to slip away alone and reconnoiter the vicinity of the wagon wreck.

He said nothing about his impending absence to anyone except Corporal Hall. To him he said only, "Sam, I'll be gone a couple of days. You'll be in charge. Be sure you keep the escorts running right. That's damned important."

Hall's curiosity showed immediately. "You going to the gold?"

"Don't ask questions," Rhett said.

"Listen, Cap'n, we're in this together and don't you forget it."

"I'm not forgetting."

"Be a big temptation for a man to want that gold for himself," Hall said.

"You getting ideas, Sam?"

Hall scowled. "I'm talking about you."

"Getting some insubordinate, aren't you?"

"Listen, you ain't an officer anymore. You ain't even a real sergeant, to my way of thinking. Rank in this bluebelly army ain't for real, far as I'm concerned."

"It's for real, as far as my orders are concerned."

"And what would you do about it if they ain't followed?"

"Sam, you're going to join up with Shelby's army, aren't you?"

The corporal hesitated, then tried to hide his hesitation. "Of course I am!"

"Shelby will give me back my rank then. Are you going to feel his army is for real?"

"Of course I will."

"Well then. You just think like it has already happened. And when I give an order, you obey. Understand?"

"Yes, suh!"

Rhett gave him a long look, but Hall met his stare. He was a good man to have with you in a fight, Rhett thought. You had to give him the benefit of the doubt.

Sherry called on Fenton at the hotel. At the clerk's call he came down at once to meet her in the small lobby. He smiled.

She did not return his smile. She did not like what she was doing.

"He is gone from the post," she said.

Fenton's smile disappeared. "When?"

She shrugged. "I don't know. I made a call at the station to check on the wounded private. Mrs. Searle told me they had not seen him since yesterday."

"Which way did he go?"

"I don't know that either," Sherry said.

"His men might know."

"Mr. Fenton, I cannot appear too inquisitive. The wounded private was the only one I could even casually question. He had no knowledge of the sergeant's whereabouts."

"Have you been able to strengthen your acquaintance with the sergeant?"

"That was my intention when I made my call this morning. Aside from a professional interest in my patient."

"Of course, of course," Fenton said, forcing another

smile, though faint. "I appreciate you doing this, Mrs.
Cowper."

There was no expression on her face.

He noted this and said, "Keep thinking about your husband, ma'am. What you are doing is a way of hitting back."

"Yes," she said. "Yes, I have talked myself into believing
that." She paused. "I'm sorry I can't give you more information."

"You have given me enough," Fenton said. "Now, if you
will excuse me, I'll take advantage of it."

"You have some idea of where he is?"

"Yes, I have some idea of where he has gone. It is my job
to learn what he is up to."

"I will try to be of more service in the future," she said.

"You are doing fine, ma'am," said Fenton. "In the memory of your gallant husband."

Because he had once done a stint as a wagon-train scout
and because he guessed where Rhett was going, Fenton was
sure he was on the right track as he headed southward
toward Sand Creek, with Fort Lyon many miles beyond.
Rhett had to be riding toward the site where he had been
accosted by Sergeant Eilers and his patrol several months
back. Though Fenton had never been there, he had a map
furnished him by Allan Pinkerton himself, appointed head
of the Union's wartime-established Secret Service.

Pinkerton's reputation as a private investigative agent
prior to the war was well established, and had led to his
selection as director of the new agency.

Fenton had worked for Pinkerton before the hostilities,
and had continued with him as the canny Scotsman went into
the government service.

As a youth, Fenton had been a trapper for a spell, tried
his hand at mining and ranch work, and had given up the
rough life when, on a visit to Chicago, he'd seen an adver-

tisement placed by Pinkerton for an operative familiar with the frontier.

He had been eastern-raised and educated until he was sixteen, when an epidemic of cholera in Saint Louis carried off his parents. An only child and now an orphan, he had offered to drive a widow's wagon in a train heading out the Oregon Trail from Independence. From then on one thing led to another until he became a seasoned westerner.

He was nearing forty now, but was still trail-tough from the jobs Pinkerton gave him. Although he affected town clothes when he had a choice, he was Pinkerton's top outdoor man, which was why he'd gotten this assignment.

Now, easy in the saddle, he rode the trail thoughtfully.

Why was his quarry going alone? The facts of this case, put together over the months starting with Sergeant Eilers's encounter with Rhett, Major Warren's report of his escape from detention at Fort Lyon, and the subsequent identification of Rhett as a Confederate officer—all this had resulted eventually in the discovery of the rebel captain's true mission, and the War Department's calling in the Secret Service to figure out a way to recover the hidden cache of contraband ingots.

Which was why Fenton wondered about Rhett being alone.

The information he had, gleaned by interrogation of certain Copperheads rounded up near Denver, was that the bullion consisted of twenty-six gold bars, weighing approximately seventy-five pounds each.

There was no way one man on a horse could carry more than two ingots. Was the rebel captain figuring to do just that and flee to Texas? A hundred and fifty pounds of gold at near $250 per pound was a sizable fortune for any man.

Somehow, though, from what he had learned by studying the captain's dossier compiled by Pinkerton, Fenton did not believe such an action fit the character of the man. Still, you could never count on what a man would do when there was gold involved.

But if the reb captain was intending to recover the entire load he'd hidden, he'd need at least a dozen men besides himself.

Fenton's mental calculations considered the detachment of troopers at the stage station. Twelve men was what Rhett had. Just enough. A coincidence? Or part of a careful plan? He remembered then that size of the detail had been specified beforehand, although Major Ronstadt at Rock Island had allowed Rhett to choose his men.

"Why not?" Ronstadt had said to Fenton during an early discussion. "We want to make it easy for him, although not so easy that he suspects he is being watched."

"Once they recover the gold, they will undoubtedly split up," Fenton had said. "Each man with his share, although the captain's will no doubt be bigger."

"We'll be ready," the major said. "We'll be watching with a force of men standing by so that no one gets away with any of it."

"Some may slip through," Fenton said.

"None will slip through," the major replied. "Our soldiers will outnumber them, and will shoot to kill without warning."

"An ambush, sir?"

"Call it that," Ronstadt said. "Or call it a massacre. Just remember these are Confederates, Fenton."

The thought came to Fenton now that perhaps the reb captain was smart enough to be satisfied with what he alone could carry. That would be close to forty thousand dollars. Ought to be enough for any man, Fenton thought.

Fenton would have to be on the alert if—and he did not know this—the gold was hidden in this area. The reb just might try to ride off alone. Hell, that would be all right. If he did, he'd reveal the location of the cache. And Fenton was an excellent shot. He'd not let the reb get away with *any* of the gold.

Rhett passed the site of the Sand Creek Massacre, no longer used by the Indians as a camp location because of its significance. He crossed the creek bed and continued south and slightly west, expecting to eventually intersect the old trail he had taken down from the mines on his aborted mission.

And eventually he did. He struck it just before it skirted the badlands into which he had plunged in desperation so many months before.

Where the wagon had been wrecked, there was now only a scattering of charred wood. He felt a momentary relief at this finding. But the relief was shortlived as he realized that Sergeant Eilers, and maybe Major Warren, had probably examined it before it was burned. Though the Cheyennes might have burned it beforehand. He hoped that was so.

Now he took the precaution of searching the surrounding terrain carefully for a sign of any watchers. He found none.

He turned his attention then to the arroyo, which in the previous late summer had been dry. Now, the thaws of spring had sent enough water down its course to change the appearance of the overburden he had collapsed to hide the gold. It looked so different that he was not sure of the exact spot.

Luckily, though, nothing had been exposed. A half million dollars lay there under the sand and gravel. And to get it to Shelby and his unvanquished southerners, he needed only shovels, and men he could trust. And nobody watching, of course.

A rumor, true or not, had come by westbound stage that Shelby was already across the border in Piedras Negras with a loyal brigade.

Rhett had failed to get the wealth to Price. He was determined to get it to Shelby. But he would have to move soon.

At that moment he suddenly had a feeling that he was being watched. Instinctively, he turned away from the arroyo, making it appear that he'd had no more than a passing interest in it. He remounted and rode back to the trail he'd taken months before, and began retracing it.

If he was being watched, let the watcher think there was no real significance in his visiting the wagon site. Let them think he was more interested in the trail farther up.

He rode with his head down, but with his eyes searching from beneath the brim of his campaign hat. And he learned then that his hunch was correct. There was a faint rising of dust from a brush-covered area that screened the trail he had taken down from Cheyenne Springs.

The dust plume was thin, almost invisible, but it was there, as of a careful rider walking his horse.

A name leaped into his mind. Corporal Hall? All the nuances of Hall's recent attitudes struck him at once. The corporal was rebellious by nature. That in itself could lead him to resentment against Rhett. Could it also lead to a faltering loyalty to the seemingly lost cause? Rhett was chagrined that he had not considered this before. From now on he'd better watch the corporal closely. God! He didn't need a mutiny on his hands now. He needed the help of every man he had.

He turned and rode toward the dispersing dust. When he reached the other trail, he saw the tracks of a horse beside those left earlier by his own. He debated then whether to follow, and decided against it. If the other rider was aware of him, the damage was done. If he wasn't, any approach could make him aware of Rhett's presence.

Who! Who might it be? A stranger? A coincidence? One of his men? He didn't know. But he was sure he had been followed.

Rhett turned back, and began his return to Cheyenne Springs.

McGregor was the only trooper in the bivouac. In answer to Rhett's questioning, he said, "The corporal went off on escort, I reckon, Sarge. Me being laid up the way I am, makes us short-handed. But I'll be ready to ride tomorrow."

"You'd better stay on sick leave a couple more days," Rhett said. He had not known McGregor before Rock Island, but had chosen him because he appraised him as an ardent southerner. He was a Virginian, and Rhett liked his attitude.

"At first I didn't understand the corporal calling you 'Cap'n,' " the trooper said. "Then he told me how he had once been in your outfit where you been a captain. It's my pleasure to serve under you, suh."

"Not captain now, McGregor. So you can drop the 'suh.' "

"I reckon it'll be 'suh' again when we get to Mexico with General Shelby."

"Maybe, Mac. We'll have to get there first."

"When will we be starting, suh—Sergeant?"

"Soon," Rhett said. "Very soon. I want to catch up with the general before he gets deeper into Mexico."

"Is he still on the border?"

"Close to it, I hear."

"Wasn't for the stage passengers, we wouldn't know much what was going on, I reckon."

Rhett nodded. "That and the telegraph line from the east to Denver. Although I understand the Injuns tear the wire down every now and then up along the Platte."

"Looks like there's a lot more Injun trouble up there than there is down here right now," McGregor said. He grinned and shrugged his wounded shoulder. "Even if they did give me this."

"They've got northern Cheyenne and some Sioux up there. From what I hear, the Cheyenne down here have so far been less trouble."

McGregor said, "Makes you wonder a little why they sent us down here instead of up there, don't it, suh?"

Rhett was thoughtful. "That it does, Mac. It surely does."

Hall rode in with the escort of the next eastbound stage. That relieved Rhett of one troubling question. But it gave him another in its place. Who had been trailing his movements down there in the area of the cache? If anyone had.

Fenton met again with Sherry, this time in an early-morning encounter on the street. It was what he had been hoping for. He had been curious to discover how her new relationship with the rebel captain was going.

He drew her aside near one of the false-front buildings that lined the roadway. "Any news for me, ma'am?"

"None. Except that he was gone for two days. And not on escort duty, either."

Fenton nodded. This he already knew, but he did not tell her so. "Anything else?"

"Nothing. Except to tell you, Mr. Fenton, that I do not like what I'm doing." She paused, then said, "After all, Sergeant Rhett was a soldier when he fought my husband— if he did. On the other side, yes, but a soldier fighting for his beliefs."

Fenton shook his head. "He was more than that, Mrs. Cowper. Before that action he was part of a Copperhead conspiracy here on the frontier. He was actually a captain on secret rebel assignment right here in Colorado Territory. He was jailed for treacherous actions, held in Fort Lyon, from where he escaped."

She looked shocked. "A captain on secret assignment? Treachery?"

"Surely you must have heard that the Confederates tried to stir up the Indians against the settlers, so as to keep Union troops from going south." He paused. "Even went so far as furnishing rifles."

"He does not seem like the kind of man who would do that," she said.

"I am telling you what is on his record."

"Records are not always accurate, are they, Mr. Fenton?"

"If he had been innocent, why would he have broken out

of Fort Lyon? I'll tell you why. He did it because he was fearful of an investigation."

A few feet away, under the porch floor of the store front, old Jim Bodine was awakened from his drunk-induced sleep of the previous night. Old Jim had once scouted for the early wagon trains along the Santa Fe Trail, and had been paid for what he knew. Now, beaten by age and liquor, he was still occasionally paid for what he knew, for bits and pieces of information that he could trade for a drink or two or three at the saloon bar.

Even befogged by hangover, his mind picked up on what he was hearing. He was sick, and needed whiskey badly. And as soon as he heard Sherry and the town stranger walk away, he wriggled out from under the boards and headed to where the whiskey was. It wasn't long before he traded what he knew about the rebel captain for what he needed, and from there the information spread fast throughout the town.

Rhett came into town because he couldn't get Sherry out of his mind. As an excuse to see her, he brought McGregor along on the pretext of having the trooper's wound looked at.

He was disappointed when he stepped into the medical office and found Craig, Sherry's father, there.

The doctor stared at him coolly and said nothing.

"Dr. Craig?"

Craig nodded.

"Sergeant Rhett, stage escort detachment. This is the man your daughter took a bullet out of a few days back. I was hoping she'd be in, so as to check up on it."

"She isn't here," Craig said coldly. He turned to McGregor. "Take off your shirt."

McGregor did so. Craig motioned him to a chair, removed the dressing, and examined the wound. He said, "There appear to be no complications. I would certify him back to duty."

"Your daughter is a very capable woman," Rhett said.

Craig lifted his eyes and stared at him again. "Tell me, why did you see the need to accompany your man here?"

"He's in my charge. And I wanted to thank your daughter personally for what she did for him."

"I'll forward your thanks to her," Craig said. "But I insist that you stay away from her in the future."

Rhett's face hardened. "Oh? And why is that, suh?"

"You know her husband was killed at Westport?"

"She told me as much."

"If you were an officer and a gentleman, Captain, you would respect her feelings, then."

"The war is over, Doctor. Has been for several weeks."

"There are some things that will never be over, Captain."

"I am now a sergeant, suh. Of the *United States* Third Volunteer Regiment."

"You were a captain in the rebel army. An officer. But not a gentleman, by God! You were an agent in a nefarious plot that can be called, at best, traitorous; at worst, inhumane— arousing Indians against those of your own race, those of your own nation."

"Where did you hear that, suh?"

"Never mind. It is now common knowledge in our town. And you will stay away from Sherry!"

Rhett's jaw tightened. The two men stared at each other. Then Rhett said, "From time to time we may need medical attention, Doctor. We have orders to protect the town if need be, as well as the stage runs. What will we do if we have more wounded?"

"*I* will be available. I refuse treatment to no one. And I hold no active animosity toward any of your men because they fought in the army of the Confederacy. However, there are many in this town who are not so forgiving. And you, sir, from what we know of your activities, are held in bitter contempt. You deny arousing the Indians against us. What were you doing then on the frontier trading from a wagon in Indian country, while carrying an officer's commission from the Confederacy?"

"I was not trading," Rhett said.

"Then what *were* you doing here?"

"I can't tell you that," Rhett said. What could he tell? That he was hauling a half million in gold?

Craig turned to Private McGregor. "You are well enough to return to your duties, soldier. Now, please leave and take your sergeant with you."

As Rhett, disgruntled, stepped out of the office, he saw a crowd gathering across the street in front of Evans's mercantile.

At the sight of him, the crowd raised their voices.

Still irked by Craig's attitude, he stopped abruptly and faced the stares of several men.

One of them called, "Get out of town, reb."

Rhett's anger flared. He called back, "This soldier was wounded fighting Injuns for you."

"It ain't him we're talking to," the man said.

Another yelled, "If you hadn't worked for the Copperheads to stir them up, maybe we wouldn't have no Injun problem."

"I have never done that."

"You saying it was never done?"

"I'm saying it was never done by me." Rhett started toward them.

Just behind him McGregor came, saying, "They're sounding mean, Sarge. We'd best be careful."

Rhett was inclined to agree. He halted halfway across and said, "You know it was Chivington's massacre that's riled the Cheyenne."

There was a silence. Then the first spokesman said, "I ain't denying that. But it don't make your own hands no cleaner."

The other man said to the crowd, "We'd ought to run the goddamn Johnny Reb out of town on a rail."

There was a murmur of assenting voices.

A woman in the crowd said, "More than one of us lost our menfolks fighting your kind."

"It was a war, ma'am."

"And Andersonville? Was that a war too? My brother died there in that filthy prison camp run by you rebs. Died of starvation."

"I had no part of that, ma'am," Rhett said. "I was a fighting soldier."

"Then what were you doing here in the Territory last year if you weren't trading guns to the Cheyenne?"

Her question stirred up a chorus of bitter comments from the others.

"Suh?" McGregor said. "Suh, hadn't we best go back to the station?"

At that moment the men in the crowd, at least ten strong, stepped forth and walked steadily toward them.

McGregor was unarmed, but Rhett was wearing a .44 army Colt in a holster. He undid the flap and drew the weapon.

The townsman who had done most of the talking was leading the others. He halted. "Pulling that gun on us, that ain't making you no friends, reb."

"Right now, this gun is my friend," Rhett said.

CHAPTER 7

RHETT was surprised when Sherry came calling at the station, ostensibly to ask for herself how McGregor was doing. He was more surprised at the friendliness of her greeting.

"I wish to apologize for my earlier rudeness. When you first arrived, I mean," she said.

"I understand, ma'am."

"I'm glad. I hope we can be friends."

"My hope too, ma'am."

At that moment Esther Searle looked from her kitchen into the main room of the station where they were conversing, and Rhett noticed the attention she was paying them, and it caused him to frown. It seemed sometimes that Esther was taking a more than passive interest in him, he thought. Nothing overt, but he had often looked up to catch her glancing his way.

It made him wonder if she was suspicious of his presence or, more probably, simply leery of him because of his Confederate background. As were all, it seemed, of the Cheyenne Springs citizens.

Including, up until now, the beautiful woman making small talk with him.

He wondered why she had so abruptly changed.

She seemed to realize this, because she said, "No doubt you are surprised at my change of feeling toward you."

"Some, ma'am," he said.

"It comes from admiration for your courageous defense of the station."

"My duty," he said.

"Yes, of course. Nevertheless, you and your men performed admirably, Sergeant."

Rhett smiled, his eyes frankly appraising her. "There is no one I would rather hear that from."

She blushed slightly, but did not seem overly flustered.

He thought, She has no doubt long ago grown used to references to her comeliness. He had a sudden desire to reach out and touch her.

For some strange reason this desire caused him to glance toward the kitchen doorway, and he caught Esther watching him from within. Her expression seemed strange to him. She had a faint knowing smile on her lips, but her eyes seemed to reflect a different mood.

A strange woman, he thought, and wondered why he was disturbed by her stare. He felt an abrupt need to get out of her sight, and to take Sherry Craig with him. Esther was intruding, he felt, and yet he was flattered rather than angered by her intrusion.

Was there something lacking in her relationship with Searle? he wondered. The thought made him turn quickly away. He went close to Sherry and led her outside.

They began to walk toward the town, and as they entered it, he was aware of the covert glances of several women who were about their business of shopping. And of a few loitering men. It did not seem to him that they had shared Sherry Craig's change of heart.

He remarked as much to her. "I was confronted earlier by some of those loafers," he said. "They've no liking for southerners."

"It will take time, Sergeant. You have to realize how angry we northerners are because the South's secession plunged us into this costly war."

His own feeling rose instantly, and he said, "From our viewpoint, we were forced to secede by the overbearing arrogance of the North."

"Please, Sergeant. Don't let's fight over it."

"No, don't let's." He was sorry he had spoken.

"I want to be your friend," she said.

"I would like nothing better. No, I take that back. I'd like to have you for more than just a friend, ma'am."

"Are all southerners so blunt?"

"No, ma'am. Just Texans." He smiled.

She said, "For now, Sergeant, friends will have to be enough."

"For now, I'll settle for that. A man gets lonely for women to talk to. All soldiers do, whatever army."

Almost the same words she had heard from Fenton! she thought, and was disturbed by this. How much of what she was doing was because of Fenton's persuasion, and how much because she found him appealing as a man, strangely fascinating to her because—she paused before saying it to herself—he was one of the enemy?

She had intended to work her way into his confidence in order to betray him. Now, suddenly, she was confused. She could not judge her own motives.

He walked her to her father's office, and stopped outside it. He saw Craig's buggy there, knew it was his by the name, followed by *M.D.,* stenciled on its side.

"It appears your father is about to make a call out of town," he said.

"Yes, he is frequently away."

"And at those times you take his place?"

"I try, Sergeant. He has taught me much, but I have a lot to learn yet." She paused. "Women doctors are not unknown on the frontier, you know."

"And is it your ambition, ma'am, to be one?"

"Possibly. Yes, I may hang out my shingle someday. A widow, Sergeant, must do one of two things. Earn a livelihood or marry again."

He wondered how it would be to have her as a wife. The thought brought a flush to his groin. But what could I offer her? he thought. I'm a Galvanized Yankee sergeant. That alone would make it impossible. *And I have a mission to perform.*

Still, he could dream. At that moment he had to fight the urge to sweep her into his arms. Instead, he took the hand she proffered, and squeezed it warmly. He saw a brief show of pleasure at this, quickly hidden. And he let himself be encouraged by it.

"I must go in," she said.

"I would like to talk to your father. When I came before, he was even more bitter than the rest."

She considered, then said, "Wait, Sergeant. You must give him more time. He was very fond of my husband. He mourns him as he would the son of his own he never had. I'm his only child, and my mother died when I was born. So his feeling about Lyle's being killed by Confederates—it almost matches my own."

She turned then and entered the office, leaving him standing there alone.

CHAPTER 8

AT that moment, from the far end of the town, a man came running up the street toward Rhett.

At first Rhett could not hear his words. Then he caught the warning: "Sergeant! Injuns!"

He got within speaking range, breathing hard, gasping out his message. "Twenty or thirty of them. Riding in from the west." He paused to catch his breath.

Rhett said, "Get to the station and send back every man of my squad you can find."

The man nodded and ran off toward the bivouac area.

Sherry heard the commotion and rushed back out of the office, followed by Craig.

Rhett said to him, "You heard?"

"I heard."

"You'd better get ready for casualties."

"My business," Craig said in a flat voice. "I'm always ready."

"I'll expect equal treatment for any of my men."

"I told you before, you'll get it." The flat tone gave way to anger.

"Just so it's understood," Rhett said.

Sherry looked from one to the other. "I'd like you two to be friends."

Craig grunted, and Rhett said, "I'm willing."

And then his troopers reached him, McGregor among them, toting his own carbine and one for Rhett, despite the stiffness in his shoulder.

Scattered shots came from the west end.

"Let's go!" Rhett said, and started toward the sound.

The reb soldiers fell in behind him, and Sherry followed.

Corporal Hall pulled up beside Rhett. "Fighting for the Yankees again, damn it."

"You forgetting what they sent us out here for?"

"I ain't forgetting what *I* came for."

"A war party of thirty Injuns could wipe out the town."

"That'd be too damn bad, wouldn't it?"

"Don't you have any feeling for your own kind?"

"They ain't *my* kind. I hate a goddamn Yankee worse than I hate an Injun. The Injuns never done me no personal harm. But there been Yankees that did."

Rhett stared between the scatter of board fronts that made up the trail town. He could see the Indians racing on now across the prairie in a widespread line of skirmish.

Armed citizens were spilling out of the buildings and taking up positions behind cover. Jed Evans was trying to organize them into some sort of defense.

As the soldiers ran up, he turned to Rhett and said, "I'm damn glad to see you, Sergeant." He paused. "They're Cheyenne, for sure. Look like maybe it's Lone Buffalo's bunch. Been a long spell since he made us any trouble. If it's him, he may have some of them Dog Soldiers with him. And they're fighting sons of bitches. He's one himself."

Evans took note then of Sherry's presence. "Sherry, get inside somewhere. It's no place for a woman out here."

She did not move from Rhett's side.

"Damn it, Sherry! Do what I say."

She still did not move.

Rhett said, "Do it, Sherry. I don't want to be worrying about you."

She hesitated for only an instant, then, without a word, ran toward the mercantile.

"Well, well," Evans said. He gave Rhett a sharp look, and scowled.

Rhett sensed the man's feelings. Well, well, yourself, he

thought. Evans was old enough to be her father and then some.

The Cheyennes were now riding a wide circle around the town.

Corporal Hall said, "A poor way to take an objective."

"They'll make a frontal attack when they're ready," Rhett said. "War to them is partly a game. They'll have to put on a show first."

Evans overheard this and said, bluntly, "If that's Lone Buffalo leading them, you can't count on anything. To him fighting is a business, what I've heard. And he's got a half-breed cousin who's turned bronco since Chivington's massacre. He thinks like a white man and acts as an adviser."

"You appear pretty well informed," Rhett said.

"A man who runs a store hears all the news," Evans said. "And all the rumors."

"I see. You believe all you hear?"

"No. Just some of it." The merchant raised his rifle and fired at one of the circling braves.

"Long range," Rhett said.

"Yeah, I know. I was just letting off steam." He turned to look at Rhett. "Every time I think the rumor about you may be true, I get that way." He paused. "Then I don't believe it, and I cool down."

The Cheyennes suddenly narrowed their circle and began a wild firing from horseback, wasting bullets.

"They're in range now," Rhett said.

The reb troopers had found protected positions, and they and the townsmen started picking targets. Two of the troopers scored hits, knocking Indians off their mounts.

"Anyhow, I'm glad you're here," Evans said. "Ain't all of us townfolks can hit a moving target."

"My men and me learned the hard way," Rhett said.

"Yeah. Against northern boys." Evans fired again, and an Indian pony went down, throwing its rider. The brave leaped up behind a companion and rode off.

"We learned against each other," Rhett said. "War is a two-edged sword."

"I don't want to see you mixing up with Sherry," Evans said. "She's been hurt enough. Don't you see how you would just aggravate her sorrow?"

Rhett felt a flare of anger, which quickly died.

There was truth in what Evans said. Every time Sherry looked at him, she'd likely see a rebel soldier pressing a trigger that fired the bullet that killed her husband.

And then, too, there was his plan to rejoin the diehard rebels under Shelby. There would be no place for her there.

Suddenly, he had no more time to think about this.

The Cheyennes turned in, as if on signal, and converged on the town, forming spokes of the imaginary great wheel they had been riding.

The defenders were besieged from all sides. Men rushed across the street to fill a perimeter, though too thinly.

Still, they halted the converging charge. Horses and riders fell as the townsmen's aim improved at shorter range.

The Cheyennes gathered in a retreat northward and halted beyond rifle distance.

"A few more charges like that and they'll really get mad," Evans said. "When they get wild and crazy, it'll get bad, real bad."

Rhett glanced at him. "You talk like you know Injuns well. How much fighting have you done against them?"

Evans flushed. "I never been a soldier," he said finally.

When Rhett made no comment on this, he said, voice rising, "But I learned about them from listening. I've heard plenty of Injun-fighters talk. Like I said, you hear a lot tending store."

"Yeah," Rhett said. "I reckon."

"Of course that don't take the place of firsthand know-how."

Rhett said nothing. For a man without actual battle experience, Evans was doing all right. Hell, out of all his men, he himself was the only one who had previously fought Injuns, he believed. It was possible that Evans's hearsay knowledge made him better informed than Rhett when it came to the Cheyennes.

As if Evans read his mind, the storekeeper said, "It's a mite strange, but I so far seen one, and only one, Dog Soldier amongst them. That's got to be Lone Buffalo himself."

Rhett recalled Zack, the stage driver, telling him about the different headdress worn by the militant warrior society. He said, "No tail feathers, eh?"

"So you know? Yeah. Another thing, their war bonnets are made of crow, not eagle, feathers."

"Hell," Rhett said, "you're a walking encyclopedia."

"For what it's worth," Evans said. "For what it's worth."

The Cheyennes charged again.

This time they raced in like cavalry, in a column and suddenly peeling off, alternately left and right, and riding to the ends of the town.

"Cripes sake!" exclaimed McGregor, who was still near Rhett. "They been army-trained?"

It was a startling sight in its precision, Rhett thought. It was an attack formation right out of the cavalry manual. *Line of troop, columns of platoons, troops wheeling left and right to flank, center firing and drawing fire.* Scaled down, of course, because of the size of force.

Somebody who knew army tactics had taught them that. Lone Buffalo? It didn't seem likely.

He had no more time to think about it. This attack came close to succeeding, reaching the very edge of town before the defenders across the street could rush back to bolster the defense.

But again the Cheyennes were beaten back.

Evans looked at Rhett. He said, "Your trooper there, he mentioned army-trained."

"Had that look," Rhett said.

Evans considered this for a long moment. Then, as if he could not hold it back, he said, "You—being a cavalry officer for the rebs—"

"So you now believe the rumor."

"I'm considering it."

"Consider away," Rhett said. He turned to McGregor. "How's the shoulder holding up, Mac?"

"All right, suh—Sarge. Lucky it was my left got hit, instead of my right. These Spencers got enough kick." He gave Rhett a searching look. "Begging your pardon, suh, but it *wasn't* you that trained them Injuns?"

"No. It wasn't me, Mac."

McGregor said, "I knew it wasn't, suh. I just knew it couldn't be."

Evans looked from one to the other of them. He said nothing.

Rhett's eye was caught then by a pony trotting up the street, behind the line of defenders. The attention of most was still on the retreated Cheyennes.

On the pony's back, slumped over its withers, was a wounded brave.

Rhett ran out and grabbed the pony by its hackamore and halted it. In his free hand he held his readied revolver.

He stared in shock, then said, "Lawler?"

The wounded brave raised his head as if with great effort. The light-skinned features with their slight Indian cast showed pain, then recognition.

"I'm Rhett."

Blood oozed from a wound in the half-breed's bared chest. He nodded, fell forward again, then tried to straighten and failed.

"It was you that taught that charge," Rhett said.

Lawler got himself erect again. "Me. I learned some things from those goddamn bluebellies that massacred us at Sand Creek." His head went down, then pulled up once more. "I failed, though, didn't I, Captain?"

Evans and McGregor came running to join Rhett. Evans lifted his rifle and took aim.

Rhett knocked the barrel aside with his hand that held his pistol. He said, "He'll make a hostage. Lone Buffalo's cousin, in fact."

"How do you know that?"

"I know."

"Well, then," Evans said, "maybe we got something here."

Rhett said, "Take his rein and tie the pony. Mac, help me get him down."

They carried the half-breed to the nearest porch and laid him out.

Evans tied the pony's rein to an adjacent hitchrack. "How bad is he hurt?"

"Got a bullet in his chest," Rhett said. "He's not bleeding from the mouth, though. Maybe nothing vital is hit."

"What you figure to do with him?"

Rhett's thought had been mostly on Lawler's condition. And on the fact that this was the man who had helped him escape from Fort Lyon. Now his mind came to the immediate concerns. "Maybe we can trade him to Lone Buffalo in exchange for leaving us alone," he said.

"We better get to dickering then. Before the Injuns hit us again."

"We can't leave him here," Rhett said. "Some damn fool will finish him off. We'll carry him out where the Cheyennes can see him."

They took Lawler to the rear of a building and propped him sitting up against the wall. Rhett took his neckerchief and handed it to him. "Hold this to stop the bleeding, George."

Evans looked startled. "First-name basis, hey? I reckon there's truth in that rumor, then."

Rhett ignored him. "We've got to parley with Lone Buffalo."

Evans said, "Who?"

"Me. I need a truce flag." He looked at the soiled white apron the storekeeper was still wearing. "That'll do."

The reb troopers had gathered around them, along with some of the townsmen. Rhett said, "Don't anybody hurt this man. I'm going to deal with the Cheyenne for him. Dead, he'll be of no use to us."

Lawler seemed to be coming out of his shock. He raised his eyes to Rhett and gave him a bitter grin. "I appreciate your concern for my health, Captain," he rasped.

"You chose your side, George. You chose to fight as an Injun."

Lawler nodded. "But not until Sand Creek," he said.

Rhett gave him a long look. Finally he said, "I think I understand." He took the apron from Evans then, and began tying it on the barrel of his carbine.

"You going out there alone, suh?" McGregor said.

"Better that way, Mac."

"I'd go with you, suh."

"Wouldn't help a bit. We'd just make two targets instead of one."

From a few yards away, and keeping a low profile as he had done all through the attacks, Fenton had watched it all and put together the picture.

He had with him a Henry .44 rifle he had recently purchased, and which he'd been using with deadly effect. It could kill at a thousand yards.

Now he walked down a few buildings and entered the Smoky Hill Trail House, where he had an upstairs room at the rear, which faced toward the group of Cheyennes gathered in the distance. He opened the window of his room and watched and listened, and saw Rhett start riding out with the improvised truce flag held high.

He felt a brief surge of respect for the blue-clad Confederate. The man had guts. But Fenton quickly conquered his feeling. In his business he had to stay clear of emotions. He had a job to do.

Rhett kept moving out, sweating heavily. Who knew what the Cheyenne Dog Soldier would do? He kept his eyes on the bunched Indians, looking for some sign, some movement.

When he thought he had gone far enough, he stopped and waved Evans's apron back and forth.

After a brief wait a lone brave detached himself from the rest and rode toward him. As he drew near, Rhett recognized Lone Buffalo. A brave warrior, all right. He did not send another into a danger zone. He came himself.

The rider halted a few paces away.

"What you want, bluebelly?"

"You remember me?"

"I remember. Then you were prisoner of other bluebellies. Now you one of them. Why?"

"It happened because of the white men's war," Rhett said.

"Hah! You lose, I hear. So you go over to other side." There was contempt in the Cheyenne's tone.

"I did not come out to talk about that."

"What you come for?"

"Look behind me. Against the building where the soldiers are. You see a wounded Cheyenne warrior?"

The Dog Soldier looked long and hard. "I see my cousin, the man who gave you help."

"He is hurt, but he will live. I will trade him to you for your word to ride away and leave this town alone."

The Cheyenne remained silent and expressionless.

"You have lost men in your attack," Rhett said. "Besides your cousin."

Lone Buffalo nodded. "Yes. Next time I bring more men. Next time I bring all Cheyenne Dog Soldiers."

"If you want your cousin to live, you must promise not to come back. Ever."

"Big promise."

"Your cousin should be worth it."

Again the Indian was silent. "It is so," he said finally. "The Cheyenne need my cousin—because he understand the lying white man's ways." He paused. "But if you lie, I come back with many Dog Soldiers. Then I will wipe this town from the earth."

"It is agreed, then?"

"It is agreed."

"I will send your cousin out."

"He can ride?"

"I will tie him on his horse."

"I wait here."

Rhett nodded and turned away.

He got back to where the others waited, gathered near Lawler.

"Well?" Evans said.

"Mac, get his pony and bring it around. We're sending him out."

Evans said, "Listen, I remember seeing this damn breed leading that last charge. Might be best to kill him."

"I've got Lone Buffalo's word to pull off his attack and leave the town alone from now on. In return for his cousin alive."

"That's different," Evans said.

"Pass the word around to your people. Tell them what's taking place."

"Sure," Evans said. "They're going to like you for what you done, Sergeant."

"Make it clear that nothing better happen to the breed."

"I will," Evans said. "I will."

McGregor brought Lawler's pony from the hitchrack. Rhett and the troopers lifted the breed onto it. Lawler, realizing what was happening, seemed to gain strength. He said, "Consider the debt you owe me fulfilled, Captain."

Rhett said nothing.

Lawler said, "You understand, Captain, why I make war now on my people's side?"

"I think so."

"I'm glad you do." The breed reached down a hand. "Good-bye, Captain."

Rhett took his hand and shook it. "Ride out careful. You lost some blood."

"Yeah." Lawler got his pony headed right and began a slow walk toward his Cheyenne cousin, waiting just beyond effective carbine range.

From his room, Fenton saw and guessed it all. He was not pleased. The bargain that he surmised had been struck would make the ex–reb captain a hero in the eyes of the town. It could delay or halt the desertion of Rhett and the recovery of the gold. Fenton was tired of waiting. He wanted to get on with his job.

He lifted the Henry rifle and took aim.

Lawler reached the waiting leader.

Lone Buffalo said in Cheyenne, "Come, cousin. I do not trust the whites. And the bluebellies least of all."

"I trust the one we helped to escape from the jail," Lawler said.

"I do not."

A rifle cracked and the half-breed toppled from his pony.

Lone Buffalo jerked his glance toward the town. A faint cloud of smoke came from a window of the hotel.

He slid off his horse, bent down over his cousin, and saw he was dead. He raised him quickly, lifted him onto his own pony, and swung up behind.

He raised his fist in defiance, then wheeled and raced out of range toward his watching warriors.

As he reached them, one said, "Do we attack again?"

"No," he said. "Not now. When I attack again, I will bring enough warriors for a massacre."

Fenton left his room and slipped out of the hotel, hoping no one had noticed him. He joined some of the townsmen who were still waiting near their battle stations, not sure what would happen next.

They had heard Rhett's warning that nothing should happen to the half-breed, and some were cursing the fool who had fired the fatal bullet.

"We find who done it, I say lynch the bastard," a man said to Fenton.

Fenton nodded agreement. He was a little shocked at the turmoil he had caused. A little fearful, even. Still, he thought he had done what should have been done. If Rhett became a respected local hero and settled down, he might forget the Confederacy and its gold.

A lesser man would not waver, but Rhett's recent actions had perturbed Fenton. Rhett was a man cast in a greater mold, he thought. A man with ideals.

He had to remember that. He had to remember always that his own priority was to make the rebel reveal the location of the bullion. That was most likely to happen if the whole town hated Justin Rhett.

It had seemed to Fenton a rational act when he had shot the breed. Now, hearing others echo the townsman's wish to lynch the shooter, he had his qualms.

He hoped to God that nobody had seen him at the window of his room. At the moment, he hoped that most of all.

The people of Cheyenne Springs did not hold Rhett to blame for what had happened. Some at first, still held by their prejudice, leaned that way. But the clearer thinking of the others spread and, despite Fenton's effort, Sergeant Rhett was aware of a change of attitude toward him when he next visited the town.

He was bitter that one of them, apparently thoughtless, had ruined his bargained truce. But for most of them he had developed a strange feeling that they had become his people, that he had a responsibility for their protection.

He was not particularly pleased with this. He cursed whatever it was in him that made him feel this way.

Now, with Lone Buffalo's threat of annihilation hanging over them, he was torn between this feeling and a sense of urgency that he must leave to join Shelby.

Corporal Hall held no such conflict of interests. Soon after the repulsed attack, he let his feeling be known once more. "I'm asking again, Cap'n. When in hell we going to make our move?"

"Getting anxious?"

"Fed up. Twice now we risked our lives for these Yankees. Just damn luck none of us got killed by them Injuns."

Irritated, Rhett said, "That's what you signed up for."

"Not me! I signed up to get out of that privy they called a prison. And with the idea of deserting at the first chance."

"The chance hasn't come yet."

"The hell you say! Ain't no reason we can't leave right now."

"Go ahead."

"How? None of us know where them ingots are."

"Then I'll say when."

The corporal's face flushed with anger, but suddenly he got a grip on himself. In a more reasonable tone, he said, "Cap'n, if anything happened to you in one of these skirmishes, that gold would be lost to the cause. Be best if you confided where it's hid."

That was something that had bothered Rhett too. But he said, "Which of you would I confide in?" He grinned slightly, knowing what Hall's answer would be.

"Why, me, of course. Ain't I second in command here?"

"I'll give it some thought," Rhett said. "Meanwhile, it's your tour to ride escort with the eastbound stage. It'll be coming in at noon."

Corporal Hall stalked off, scowling.

CHAPTER 9

RHETT saw Sherry again two days later.

He had walked into town to make a purchase at Jed Evans's store, and met her as she was coming out with an armload of groceries.

"I've something I want to discuss with you, Sergeant," she said. "I intended to call again at the station, but now that you are here, I must see you alone."

"My pleasure," Rhett said, smiling.

She did not return his smile. She seemed ill at ease. "There is no one in my father's office now. Will you come with me?"

He nodded, although her worried expression bothered him. He took the groceries from her arms, and they crossed the street. They entered Craig's place, and she gestured for him to put down his burdens on a chair.

At that moment a woman screamed out on the roadway. The sound was followed by a burst of rifle fire from the west end of the street.

They rushed to the front window and saw the woman lying in the dust.

There was another burst of firing, and bullets kicked up spurts of dust from around where the woman lay. Sherry cried out a single word: "Justin!" She had never called him by his first name before.

He was already at the door. He jerked it open, glanced once toward where the shots had come from, then crouched and ran for the woman's inert form. He straightened with

her in his arms, turned and rushed back through the doorway to lay her on Craig's examining table.

Rifle fire sounded again, mixed with the tinkle of breaking
glass. Sherry had moved to the table, and he heard her say,
"There's no blood!" And then he was again at the door and
passing through to the street.

Behind him he heard her again call out, "Justin!" It gave
him a heady feeling that brought recklessness to his next
action. He began running up the street toward the rifleman's
position.

A shot splintered a wood awning support post at his
shoulder, and he ducked into a throughway between two
structures and came out behind the row of false-fronts.

When a lull came in the shooting, he continued his way
west. He's reloading, thought Rhett. Must have got off more
than a dozen shots. Possibly has a sixteen-shot Henry rifle.
The rifle the Confederates called "that damned Yankee rifle
that can be loaded on Sunday and fired all week!"

With some wryness, he touched his holstered army Colt.
He'd play hell getting close enough to use it, he was thinking.

He was halfway up the line of structures when the firing
resumed. Now it seemed wild and aimless, as the sounds
came to him of windows being shot out, bullets ricocheting
off an iron wagonwheel rim, wood splintering, and all mixed
with the cries of frightened women and the hoarse shouts of
men.

Somebody has gone crazy, he thought. Crazy or drunk.
Or both.

A man in a barkeep's apron hailed him from the back door
of a saloon. "Sergeant!"

Rhett paused and gave him a questioning look.

"You got to do something," the saloon man said. "Old
Jim Bodine's got himself a rifle and he's shooting up the
town."

"Jim Bodine?"

"Town drunk," the barkeep said. "Used to be a top scout—till likker done him in. Reckon the old bastard has got a case of the d.t.'s again. Happened once before. Got to thinking everybody was a hostile Injun."

"Hell!" Rhett said.

"Yeah," the barkeep said. "And then some."

A shot blasted, and glass shattered at the front of the saloon. "Damn!" the barkeep said, and disappeared inside.

Rhett sprinted now, toward the end of the town.

Before he reached it, he cut back through the buildings to study the street, taking care not to expose himself.

The last structure of the town, set apart by seventy-five feet of open space, was the small wooden church. A faint side road angled through the space to the town cemetery behind it. Despite its size, the church boasted a bell tower, complete with bell.

Rhett studied the bell tower for several seconds before he saw the rifle barrel poking out over the waist-high sill of one of the open sides.

The rifle belched smoke, and shots raked the street. A horse tied to a hitchrack went down, kicked a couple of times, then lay still.

A blood-curdling yell came from the belfry, and an unkempt figure in filthy buckskins stood up in plain sight.

Rhett was too far away for accuracy, but he drew his Colt, shot high, and heard a clang as his bullet struck the hanging bell.

The response was instant. Bodine's rifle muzzle swung and a slug slammed into the corner of the building above Rhett's head, tearing off a long splinter of board.

The old man, crazed as he might be, handled that rifle well. Too damned well.

Rhett had to get closer. Momentarily, he wondered why none of the townsmen had yet taken up arms to try to dislodge the sniper. Damned slow to react, he thought.

And he thought, too, of the woman he had seen fall after

the first volley, the unconscious body he had laid on the medical table for Sherry to attend. It was luck that Sherry herself had not been a target moments before. His anger rose at the senseless shooting, and he searched about for some cover to protect his advance.

There was only the cemetery, which he might reach by circling fast from behind the structures beyond him. A half dozen granite headstones stood at random among the simple wooden markers. Deceased prominent citizens, he decided.

He slipped to the back of the structures again, took a deep breath, and made a dash for the burial ground.

Old Bodine immediately opened fire, coming godawful close. Only Bodine's bad eyesight could have saved him, Rhett thought as he reached one of the stone memorials and fell prone behind its meager protection. Bad eyesight due to age and maybe bad whiskey.

He was close enough to use his revolver, but it held only four shots now, and he carried no reloads. And he was still a hundred feet from the church, and Bodine had come around on the side of the belfry that faced him.

Bodine suddenly withdrew his rifle and stepped back for no apparent reason. Crazy! Rhett thought, and sprang up and raced twenty feet to the next monument. Bodine was exposed again. Rhett risked a shot, missed, and struck the bell, while Bodine ricocheted a shot off the top of the marker inches above Rhett's head. Three shots left in his revolver, Rhett remembered, and cursed his miss.

After Bodine's next shot, Rhett took a chance and raised his head. He saw the old derelict crouching to reload his weapon.

Rhett took advantage of it, sprang to his feet and reached another chunk of inscribed granite. He had the wild thought that his own life could depend on the number of prominent citizens buried in the plot.

The rifle barrel appeared over the belfry banister, and Rhett flung a shot at the boards enclosing it. He saw the barrel jerk back and heard old Bodine scream like a panther. The sound was enough to raise the hairs on his neck. He still did not know if he'd wounded the man, or if the old bastard was just giving his insane war cry. Two shots left now; he couldn't waste any more, and old Bodine likely had a full magazine again.

Where the hell were the others? Why didn't somebody from the town side him? His anger drove him to a desperate run for the rear door of the church, and strangely, Bodine did not fire. Maybe I got him with that last shot, he thought.

He twisted the knob of the door, it opened, and he stepped inside and found himself in a room with an open door beyond. He reached the door and looked out over the rows of pews facing it. Beyond, at the front, between two doors set a few feet apart, there was a ladder mounted on the wall. It led up through a trap opening in the floor of the belfry.

A rope dangled through a small hole near the access, its end within reach of the church floor.

His first thought was to rush for the ladder, but he discarded that the moment he saw Bodine's rifle poke down through the trap, covering the full length of the rungs.

He stayed to one side and maneuvered his way to the bell rope, as Bodine triggered an aimless burst that ripped holes in the church floor. He reached for the rope and grasped it.

It took two hands to pull the weight of the bell, and his right still clutched his Colt. He managed, even so, to toll it, with a desperate hope the noise would drive the old man to drop his weapon.

But the tug on the rope tightened his finger on his own trigger and blasted a shot vertically through the belfry floor.

A second later old Jim Bodine's body tumbled headfirst through the open trap and smashed the floor at Rhett's feet, audibly snapping the scrawny neck.

Vomit rose in Rhett's throat. He stood there swallowing to keep it down.

In a few minutes he heard feet pound against the entrance stoop, one of the doors was flung open, and three or four men burst through. Rhett raised his eyes to theirs, and was shocked at the anger he saw there.

The first to speak was the barkeep who had earlier shouted at him to do something. Now the man raged, "Did you have to kill him?"

Rhett was stunned by the words. Then he said, "He had to be stopped. He shot a woman in front of the doctor's office."

One of the others scowled. "Trigger-happy, ain't you? Like all the rest of you Johnny Rebs. That woman wasn't hit. She only fainted."

Rhett turned away then, and let the vomit come.

He was back with Sherry in her father's place.

She said, "I'm sorry, Justin. I tried to call after you, but I wasn't sure myself, even though I saw no blood. It was several minutes before she came around."

"Godammit!" he said. "What did they want? It was only luck he *didn't* kill her. Or somebody else. The man was insane, shooting up the town."

She put her hand on his shoulder. "I know. You acted the way a man should in the situation. Bravely. When I think how bravely, I detest myself."

"Why?" he said. "*Why?*"

"Because—" She tried to get the words out, but couldn't. And then she realized he was referring to the reaction of the people of the town, and she was afraid to reveal her spying for Fenton to him when he was already deeply hurt.

"Why?" he said again.

"They'll get over it, Justin. It's because, disreputable though he was, he was a figure here. A great frontiersman, and a man admired in his time. For that, the town tolerated him for years. He was even not punished when he got wild once before with delirium tremens and . . . did this. I think they'll realize later that you saved some of their lives. Give them a little time to get over the passing of a familiar being. They tolerated him with . . . a kind of contemptuous affection."

"It's because I'm a southerner," he said.

She nodded. "Yes, that too."

"And you? How do you feel?" His question was roughly spoken, the first time he had ever addressed her so.

She had both of her hands on his shoulders now. "How do I feel? I feel I want to call you by your first name, Justin. Does that tell you anything?"

He grabbed her in his arms, and held her with his lean jowl pressed against the smoothness of her cheek.

She didn't resist.

The door opened, and Doc Craig stepped in.

It was a moment before either of them was aware of his presence.

"Get out!" Craig said.

Rhett loosened his embrace and whirled about.

"There was a shooting here, father," Sherry said. "And—"

"I heard," Craig snapped, still facing Rhett. "Get out, I said!"

"Go, Justin," Sherry said. "Please, for now."

Rhett looked at her and saw the pleading in her eyes. He nodded, and turned and left without a word.

CHAPTER 10

MCGREGOR came to the bivouac area and said to Rhett, "Suh, that lady doctor, Miz Sherry, she's in the station asking to see you."

Pleasure showed on Rhett's face before he hid it.

McGregor grinned. "A fine lady, suh. Can I tell her you'll be there?"

"Not necessary," Rhett said. "I'll tell her myself."

He entered the main room of the station, and Sherry rose from a chair and came toward him. She took his arm. "Might we walk?"

"Why not?"

Once outside, she said, "There are things I have to tell you, Justin."

Her tone caused him to wonder, but he waited.

"I . . . I find this hard to say. A confession, really."

"A confession, Sherry?"

"Yes." She hesitated, searching for the words. "I've not been honest with you."

"In what way?"

"I have been a spy."

"A spy? Where?"

"Here. With you. I have been reporting things you've told me. To a man."

"A man?" He looked sharply at her.

"There is a man staying at the Trail House. Some sort of secret agent for the government."

He considered this in silence. Then he said, "And why would you be reporting to a secret agent?"

"Forgive me, Justin." There was pleading in her eyes.

"Why?"

"Because I'm sorry. I—"

"I mean why were you doing this?"

"When you came here—at the beginning—it was because of Lyle . . . my husband." She paused to recover her voice. "You don't know how it is for a widow whose man has been killed in battle. The hate that festers for the enemy who caused his death." She was clutching his arm as if he would pull away.

He put his hand over her gripping fingers. "I think I know," he said.

"He played on my hate," she said. "He spoke of how it was the one way I could strike back at those who had killed Lyle. And I felt I was doing that—at first."

He kept holding her hand under his. "And now?"

"Now? Everything has changed. Don't you know my feelings toward you are different?"

"If they are, I'm glad," he said.

"They are, Justin, they are."

"Who is this agent?"

"His name is Fenton. He arrived here right after you did. He is living at the hotel."

"Fenton?" he said. "Describe him to me."

"A tall man, rugged-looking. Looks like a rancher in town clothes."

Rhett's recall went back to one of the earliest arrivals from the east. "I remember him."

"He is the one who started those terrible rumors about you."

"How do you know?"

"He told them to me."

He withdrew his hand. "And you, did you tell your father?"

"I told no one, Justin, believe me. I couldn't."

"Why?"

"I just couldn't. I know you wouldn't have done what he said. I know you wouldn't have given weapons to the Indians to kill whites."

"Then why did you wait to tell me this?"

"My feeling for you didn't change overnight. You have to understand that."

"So you were playing a game, at first?"

"Yes, I was playing a game."

"And now?"

"Would I be telling you this if I still were?"

He took her hand again.

She said, "I *had* to tell you, Justin." She raised her eyes to his.

He was startled at the invitation there. He kissed her as she raised her lips. It had been a long time since he'd done that to a woman.

He said, "You know how I feel."

"Tell me."

"No."

"But why?"

"Would it be fair? To you, I mean. You have lived less than a year with your husband's death. Can you forget?"

Her pleasure left her, and a sadness returned. "It is a thing I live with. I loved him so, Justin. I can never forget the love we had."

"Can you forget your hate against his enemy?"

"I'm trying," she said. "I'm trying hard."

"All right then," he said.

She offered her lips again, and he met them, and then he was holding her in his arms, tightly, thrusting his body against hers, his want beyond his control.

"Justin, not here!" But she did not try to pull away.

Her words, though, brought him around. He glanced over her shoulder and saw Esther Searle at a window of the station, watching. There was a smile on Esther's face.

He said shakily, "We'd better walk."

"Yes," Sherry said. "We'd better."

They turned down toward the river, and when they reached it they strolled along its bank, eastward away from the town.

He said, "Tell me what you know about this agent."

"Very little. He said the government suspected you of treason, that you were a diehard who they thought might still be loyal to the South. That you were under surveillance for that reason."

"I guess it's natural that us Galvanized Yankees are always under suspicion."

She did not speak for a moment, as if the subject on her mind was one she found difficult to voice. Then she said, "He said something else. He said that you had been with the rebels at Westport."

Rhett's face hardened.

"Justin, is it true?"

He hesitated.

"Is it?"

"Yes."

"Oh God!" Almost involuntarily, she freed her arm from his. "It could even have been you who killed him!"

"There were hundreds of us mixed in the cavalry battles," he said.

"But it could have been."

"I said before, it was war, and he was a soldier."

They had stopped. He looked at her and she did not meet his eyes. "Oh God!" she said again. "When I think that, it seems to change everything."

He moved toward her, reached out gently and drew her into his embrace. "I wish that wasn't so," he said.

"I'm so afraid," she said. "So afraid it will be between us—always. Always, Justin."

Still, she did not try to free herself.

His blood began to pound. His arms tightened around her, and he kissed her savagely.

She did not struggle, and suddenly she was returning his fire with her own.

They were in a small clearing surrounded by river brush. And in a moment they were lying in the sand. His hands fumbled with her garments. Hers unfastened his.

Afterward they lay side by side, Rhett relaxed and replete, his eyes closed. Then gratitude for his relief flooded him, and he rolled up on a shoulder and leaned to brush a gentle kiss across her mouth.

She had been staring at the sky, and turned her face away from his. "Don't, Justin. Don't. Not now."

He was surprised. It was a time for tenderness, he thought. Every woman he'd ever had wanted those intimate moments of tenderness afterward.

She rolled away from him and got to her feet, rearranging her clothing. "Take me back to the station," she said.

"I'm sorry," he said, not knowing what else to say. "I thought you wanted it as much as I."

"Do you have to talk?" she asked. "Take me back."

He stood up and buckled his belt. "If that's what you want," he said.

She started walking toward the station, not speaking.

"Will you tell me what's wrong?"

Instead of a reply, she took his arm.

"That's better," he said.

They walked a few paces in silence.

Then she said, "I'm sorry, Justin. About the way I feel now, I mean. I'm all mixed up."

"I wouldn't have done it if you had resisted."

"I didn't want to resist. Not then."

"Well?"

"It was Lyle," she said. "Afterward, it was Lyle. Don't you see?"

"No."

"When you took me, when you were making love to me, I forgot him. For once he was out of my mind."

"And then?"

"And then—afterward—he came back. He came back more strongly than ever. It was like he was accusing me. Not of adultery. Not that. But of being traitorous to his memory. Of consorting with his enemy." She turned her head to look at his profile and saw the grimness there. "Justin, do you understand?"

"I understand you're wrong," he said. "You're wrong in keeping the memory of his death always with you. He's gone, and you've got to get on with your living. You've got to forget."

"If I only could!" she said. "No. No, I'm not certain I want to. That's the worst part of it all."

Rhett encountered Fenton when the latter came to the station to take passage on the westbound stage to Denver.

He had decided he would not reveal he was aware of his surveillance. He would not jeopardize Sherry by arousing any suspicion in the agent.

As to Sherry, he had not seen her for two days, not since she had clasped his hand in a quick good-bye and walked alone into town. There had been tears in her eyes when she left, but she had not looked back. And he had taken this as a sign that she did not want to see him, for a while at least. He would not press her. She had a problem that only she could solve.

Now, as Fenton waited for the stage, Rhett engaged him in conversation.

Fenton greeted him casually, then said, "Fine job you did a few days ago, Sergeant. Without the help of you and your men, we'd not likely have beat off those redskin raiders."

"That's our job, suh."

"Lucky for us," Fenton said with a smile.

"You have the look of a western man," Rhett said. "This your first skirmish with Indians?"

Fenton was slow to answer. Then he said, "Well, no. I have scouted a bit for wagon trains in my time. Up the Oregon Trail."

"And now?"

"Between jobs, so to speak. Just looking the country over."

"Not much going on in Cheyenne Springs," Rhett said.

"I have come to that conclusion."

"Be a lot more going on up Denver way, was a man looking."

"Happens to be where I'm heading now," Fenton said.

"The westbound should be along anytime now."

"Yeah. Well, I want to compliment you again on your conduct during the attack."

"Too bad somebody ruined the truce," Rhett said. "I passed the word to let the breed go free."

Fenton shrugged. "Don't blame yourself, Sergeant. Somebody didn't hear the word apparently. Somebody with an itchy trigger finger."

"I don't remember seeing you around during the fight," Rhett said. "Did you get the word?"

"I sure did, Sergeant. I was down the street a ways from where you were. But I got the word."

"You didn't see the shot fired, by any chance?"

"I surely didn't," Fenton said. "The sound came from up the road from where I was. That's all I can tell you."

Rhett said, "Thinking back, it seems to me the sound came from near the hotel."

"I was several doors down," Fenton said. "But it didn't sound like it to me."

"Had to be a fair shooter. The breed was at a far range for most of the townsmen."

"Yeah, he was. Lucky shot, I reckon."

"Unlucky, I'd call it."

"Of course. I didn't mean that the way it sounded," Fenton said.

It was an unscheduled stage run, and the westbound pulled in to use the station only as a swing stop. Still, there was considerable stir as the hostlers changed the teams, and several passengers went around to use the rear privies.

Rhett was still there when the coach pulled out again. He watched it head through the town, and wondered what business Fenton had in Denver. It occurred to him that the telegraph was there, the line from the east following the Platte.

A loiterer from town watched too. He was at Rhett's elbow. Now he said, "Sergeant?"

Rhett turned.

"I overheard you talking to the stranger. About the killing of that breed."

"Yes, suh?"

"What he said about where he was, that ain't so. I seen him come out of the hotel carrying a Henry rifle. Hell, you could knock a man down a long ways off with one of them, couldn't you?"

Esther Searle called to Rhett while he was still considering what the loiterer had told him.

"If you have the time, Sergeant, I made extra dessert. There's some left. If you'd be interested."

He had things on his mind other than eating, and he was about to decline her offer.

"I'd welcome a chat with you," Esther said.

She made it hard for him to refuse. He admired her. She worked hard and he had never heard her complain. He put all thought of Fenton out of his mind, and walked to where she stood just inside the door.

"In the kitchen, Sergeant," she said. "It'll be easier there."

He wondered a little at her words. The main room was vacant. The whole station appeared empty. But he followed her to the kitchen and saw she had set two places on a small table with servings of a fresh-baked pie.

She gestured to a chair and went to the big range to get coffee for him.

"This is mighty nice of you, ma'am," he said. "We eat well enough at our own camp mess, but we don't get too fancy with our Dutch oven out there."

She filled his cup and hers, and sat opposite to him. At the small utility table, he was aware of her nearness. With another man's wife—a handsome one, too—he was embarrassed at her closeness.

She did not seem to be bothered by it.

There was a lot of prettiness left in her, he thought. And hard work had not yet worn out her body. Rather, it had kept her trim. It had kept her breasts high and firm, that was certain. Looking at her, only an arm's reach away, disturbed him.

What had happened down there by the river with Sherry had aroused in him interests long held dormant by necessity.

"I don't know what we would have done without you recently," she said. "With the Indians and all, I mean."

"I guess it was fortunate that we got here when we did, ma'am."

"Please, Sergeant. Call me Esther."

"I'm not sure your husband would care for that."

"No, I guess not. But I meant *now*—while we're sitting here chatting."

"If it would please you, ma'am—Esther."

"It would, very much—Justin."

"Why?"

"A woman gets lonely, Justin, in a place like this."

"Lonely? With people coming in and out on the stages all the time?"

"People without faces, without names. Strangers. We have no friends. We have no time for friends."

"I reckon it does get hard for a woman."

She was silent.

He sipped at his coffee. The hunger in him was not for food.

"I saw you with Sherry," she said suddenly.

"I know."

She smiled. "I'm sorry that caused you to leave."

He grinned faintly. "It all worked out."

"Yes, I'm sure it did." She tossed her head slightly. "I was only sorry because I enjoyed seeing the two of you paired. It was very exciting to watch."

"To see a man kiss a woman?"

"For me, it was. Oh, it was! To see *you* kiss her."

"I'm not sure I know what you mean, ma'am."

"You know," Esther said. "I'm sure you do."

He wasn't quite sure, but he thought he did. It aroused him. He said, "I'm sure, Esther, that being the attractive woman you are, you've had your own share of kissing—from your husband."

Her face showed him nothing. "We have been married five years, Justin."

"Even so," he said.

"No," she said. "Not even so."

"I find that hard to believe."

"I'll take that as a compliment. But have you ever been married?"

"No, ma'am. I reckon the war has kind of interfered with that."

"You are a fine-looking man," she said. "You need a woman."

"I'm still a soldier," he said. "I could not support a wife."

Her eyes searched out his and held them boldly. "I wasn't speaking of marriage," she said.

"I don't trifle with other men's wives, ma'am."

She took that in silence, then suddenly sighed. "Of course. I should have guessed." She paused. "I hope you won't think me a loose woman, Justin. I have never said these things before to any man.''

He started to say he understood, then realized what a vain fool that would make him sound. He said, "We all have our vagrant thoughts sometimes, I reckon.''

"Vagrant,'' she said. "Yes, that's it.'' She paused again. "You and Sherry make a handsome couple. Will you marry her?''

"As I said, I'm a soldier. My prospects are worse than poor, being in an enemy army, so to speak.''

"But you'll be mustered out before long, now that the fighting is over.''

"I don't know when.''

"She will wait for you, if you want her.''

"And just how do you know that?''

"I am a woman, Justin. That's how I know.''

"Why are you telling me this?''

"All women are matchmakers at heart,'' she said.

"Even you?''

"Even me. Some women can take their pleasure vicariously that way.''

"Is it enough?''

"No, Justin, it isn't enough.''

"I'm sorry.''

A faint, resigned smile touched her lips. "We are both sorry, then.'' She got up from the table and moved to the cooking range. She said, over her shoulder, "Eat the dessert, Justin. That's what I offered you. Surely, you have no scruples against doing that?''

Rhett's conversation with Esther lingered with him.

That he could be aroused by her boldness so soon after he had made love to Sherry bothered him. And yet it led him to make a decision.

He would take his men and make his move to join Shelby.

There would be other women, in other times, in other

places. Esther had made him aware of that. He had lived to over thirty years of age without a permanent tie to one woman. He could go on that way, a way most men in the West did.

It was best for Sherry. He knew that now. When the early days of passion wore off, the intrusion of her slain husband would return.

She would suffer guilt, and that would bring back her hate for the Confederacy, he thought. She could never forget that he, Rhett, had been one of the enemy. It would always be between them. He could not put her into a life like that. It was best that she forget him. It was best that he forget her.

CHAPTER 11

SERGEANT Eilers of the 1st Colorado Cavalry, the noncom who had brought Rhett into Fort Lyon the previous year, was now a lieutenant.

Ever since the ex–reb captain and his Galvanized Yankees had taken up escort duties at Cheyenne Springs, Lieutenant Eilers had been making plans of his own.

He had been ordered to Bugle, the next home station west of the Springs. There were five swing stations, or a distance of a little under sixty miles, between them. He had been placed on alert for a quick move of the platoon under his command. To date, his tentative objective remained the area around where the reb's wagon had broken down.

Eilers had been interrogated by agents from the War Department several times. This after Major Warren had made his report of the suspected gun-running of the escaped prisoner. Gradually, Eilers had pieced together that the department's interest was in more than a mere conspiracy to arouse Indians.

He had found no real evidence at the wagon of such activity, and had so reported to Warren.

He had forgotten the matter then, until rumors the Secret Service was involved in the investigation began to grow. Major Warren had lent some credence to the rumors before resigning his post to become Indian agent on the Arkansas.

The particular interest that later investigators seemed to have in Eilers's description of the false bottom built into the wagon brought him around finally to the suspicion that they were really looking for *gold*.

His contact still later with Fenton reinforced his suspicions. Fenton was evasive, and all Eilers really knew was that he was to cooperate fully with the agent.

But he began to read between the lines. He knew that the ex–reb captain was at the Springs for more than routine escort duty.

Eventually, he concluded he had been a fool. That he had quite possibly at one time been near to a sizable fortune in bullion, had he only known where to look. He wouldn't miss out on it this time, government or no government.

He had a core of men in his platoon that he could trust. Trust, that is, to disregard the law or military authority except his own. He had drawn them from the dregs of Denver. Many were mustered-out veterans of Sand Creek's Bloody 3rd. He had wangled their reenlistment into his platoon, with promises that they could all soon be living a life of ease across the border in Mexico. Once there, Eilers had plans to cut down his force drastically. If he shared at all, it would be with only a few.

When the agent, Fenton, got off the Denver stage at Bugle, Eilers knew the time was getting close. Fenton said, "Take your men to White Horse and be ready."

White Horse was the midpoint swing station between Bugle and Cheyenne Springs.

"I'll be back in a couple of days," Fenton said. "As soon as I can wire my report to the department, you may have orders to stake out the ambush for those secesh."

"How soon?"

"Very soon, I'd say."

Fenton got back on the stage and continued west.

Eilers immediately pulled the hardcases of his platoon off escort duty. He'd leave the rest behind to carry on.

He was glad the wait was almost over. He looked forward to the coming action.

When he reached White Horse with his men, he demanded, and got, fresh horses. They spent a night in bivouac, but on alert. Eilers's nerves were on edge. He had the feeling that even now he should be heading south.

He was sure of it when Zack Handy roared in next morning with the next westbound. The stagedriver got off the box cussing, and loud enough to rouse the station.

"Goddamn Johnny Rebs!" Zack yelled. "They deserted the Springs! Left us high and dry without no escort. I been on edge the whole run, seeing Cheyennes in my head behind every bush."

"Deserted?" Eilers said. "When?"

"Just before I pulled out. And said nary a word to nobody."

Eilers wasted no more time listening. His men were equipped and ready, and within a half hour they were on their way.

He knew that the government considered the wagon site the key to finding where the gold was hidden. He knew because Fenton had finally admitted it when Eilers was briefed on setting up the ambush in the surrounding *malpaís*.

The rebs had several hours' start on him, but he was twenty-five miles closer. He'd beat the rebs there and be waiting.

Fenton had made a quick contact by wire with his superiors and started immediately back with orders to move.

By the time he reached White Horse, Lieutenant Eilers and his men had left. He was angered that the Coloradan had not waited for the orders. Still, learning the reason from a hostler, he had to admit the lieutenant used good judgment.

The hostler said, "Old Zack come in here screaming on account he didn't have no escort out of Cheyenne Springs. Said them Galvanized Yankees had deserted. The lieutenant, he didn't waste no time. Went after them, I reckon."

He debated whether to take a horse and follow Eilers, but

decided there was no real reason to do so. Eilers had been briefed on what was expected of him.

He had been briefed to let the rebs uncover the gold, then take it from them. If that meant wholesale killing, so be it. Fenton felt considerable qualms about that. But he was only following orders. That was it. Only following orders.

Fenton continued on the stage to Cheyenne Springs.

He was surprised when he debarked there and found Sherry just leaving the station. Esther Searle accompanied her as she emerged from the place. Sherry seemed distraught, and her eyes looked as if she had been crying.

Fenton tipped his hat to the ladies, then drew Sherry aside as Esther went back inside.

"You appear upset, Mrs. Cowper." He had never seen her like this before.

She suddenly blurted, "They're gone! All of them. Even Justin!"

"Justin?" Fenton's eyebrows raised.

"Rhett. Captain—Sergeant Rhett."

"So," Fenton said, "they deserted."

"Do you know where they have gone?"

He was struck by the urgency in her voice. He said, "Do you care?"

"I'm asking."

He searched her face, again noting her ravaged eyes. He said, "You *were* play-acting in leading him on, weren't you?"

"Of course," she said.

He knew then where she stood. Intuitively, he could tell. An anger arose in him at that moment. Women! he thought, as disdain flooded through him. You could not depend on them, he thought. He was seeing an example of that now. She had become emotionally entangled with the man she was supposed to watch.

She had done so despite the widow's grief he had counted on to bar this. It irked him that he had misread her.

Worse, she had been disloyal to her husband, and that

turned Fenton's anger into rage. He suddenly wanted to lash out at her, and he said coldly, "Since you were only play-acting, you will be glad to know he is at this moment riding into an ambush. And, I might add, it will be where they once found the wagon he lost during his arrest for inciting Indians."

"Near Fort Lyon? Why would he go there?"

Fenton realized he had said more than a man of his profession should have done. "I can't tell you that," he said.

Perfidious woman, he thought. I should never have sought her help. He turned away and stamped off toward the town and his hotel.

She followed him at a distance, then went on to the livery and rented a horse. She returned to her home and quickly changed into riding clothes.

She was not certain where she was going, but she knew that Justin had to be riding toward Fort Lyon. She took the trail leading there. She knew, though, that she could never overtake him. He had too much of a start.

Rhett and his twelve southerners rode at a trot.

All the men seemed eager and excited that finally they were on their way to carrying out their plans.

Corporal Hall rode at Rhett's side, no longer wearing a scowl. "By God! Cap'n, this is the best I've felt since we had Blunt's bluebellies on the run across Missouri!"

The corporal's mood was infectious. Rhett's own blood was aroused by once more having an objective. He shoved all thoughts of Sherry from his mind.

He looked back at his men, riding in a column of twos, each with twin saddlebags and some with short shovels he had found and taken from a shed at the stage station. It bothered him that he'd stolen them. But you couldn't dig up gold with your fingers.

And each saddlebag would hold an ingot.

Twenty-six gold bars for Shelby's force. He'd let nothing stop him now. Nothing.

Lieutenant Eilers selected an area to picket the horses among some sand hills in the badland area. He rode closer to the charred remnants of the wagon and hurriedly picked hidden positions within carbine range, placed his men there, posted lookouts to watch for approach of the rebels, and settled down for a short wait.

He made certain that each man knew he was not to shoot until Eilers gave a signal. Let the rebs dig up the gold first. There must be no warning to the rebs.

Later he would annihilate them. He could not leave survivors to track them as they fled with the loot toward the border.

Corporal Hall, still riding beside Rhett, had subsided into deep thoughtfulness after his first expression of satisfaction at leaving their escort duty behind.

Twice Rhett gave him a studying glance, but said nothing. Rhett had things on his own mind.

At long last, Hall said, "Cap'n, you ever think of taking that gold for your own self?"

"Don't even think about it," Rhett said. "That's Confederate gold."

"Well now, that depends how you look at it, seems to me. Where'd it come from? It came from northern mines. Most likely stole from northern miners over a period of time. Stole by what the Yankees call our Copperheads." Hall paused. "I'd say that makes it more rightly called Yankee gold."

"What're you trying to say, Sam?"

"I'm trying to say there'd be no harm in taking that *Yankee* gold, the war being over and all, and keeping it for our own selves."

"You forget one thing," Rhett said. "The war isn't over, not for us. Not if we join up with Shelby and carry on."

Corporal Hall scowled. He rode awhile in brooding silence. "The hell with Shelby!" he said finally. "I say we done our part. I say let's look out for us. We split up the gold and we are all each fixed for life."

Rhett made no reply, and Hall said, "You going to tell me you never thought of that? You going to tell me an officer is above all that?"

No, Rhett thought, he wouldn't tell Hall that. He *had* thought about it. Back there with Sherry, he had thought about it a lot.

"I seen a lot of army life these past four years," the corporal said. "And I seen a lot of officers and taken their crap. An officer, he puts his pants on the same way as an enlisted man. Don't try to tell me no different."

"We both fought," Rhett said slowly. "And if we give up now, we fought in vain. We've got one chance left to salvage something for the South. To force more honorable terms than have been granted. If we don't, if Shelby fails, we'll be at the mercy of northern politicians for years to come."

"To hell with the years to come!" Hall said. "We done our part. If it wasn't enough, let's salvage something for ourselves." He paused. "That's my way of looking at it, Cap'n."

Again Rhett made no reply.

"Goddammit!" Hall said, "this Shelby puts his pants on the same way too! How do you know he won't take that gold and buy himself the good life down there in Mexico?"

"I do not believe that," Rhett said. He couldn't let himself believe it. If he did, there was nothing left.

"I tell you what, Cap'n. You think on this. You think on it real good."

Rhett said, "I'd guess you've talked this up some with the others?"

"That I have. I surely have."

"And?"

"And near half agree. And the rest are coming around."

His own idealism had betrayed him, Rhett thought—

perhaps because he'd failed in his original mission. But he had tried to pick men who shared his loyalty to the South.

He had begun earlier to suspect Hall, but he had underestimated the man's influence, it appeared. That and the treacherous fascination of wealth.

These were all men who had willingly offered their blood for an ideal, but they balked at offering gold.

Well, he would not turn back now. He'd lead them to the cache, and he'd take his chance on regaining their loyalty. But Corporal Hall and he went back together a long way. Once Hall had saved his life. He did not know now what he would have to do about Hall.

And just then he saw the Indians. Corporal Hall saw them too.

They were off in the distant southwest, and angling northeasterly. A large war party, Rhett guessed, of at least fifty braves.

"Jesus!" Hall said. "You think they seen us?"

"They must have," Rhett said. "But they're not after us. They're heading direct for Cheyenne Springs."

"Good! Just so they leave us alone. Let them damn Yankees see how well they do without us rebs to help them."

"He said they'd be back," Rhett said. "But I didn't think it would be this soon."

"Who?"

"Lone Buffalo, that Dog Soldier chief."

"Yeah. He was some put out about one of them Yanks killing his cousin."

"This changes things."

"They ain't turning toward us."

"I'm thinking of the town."

"Dammit!" Hall said. "We're on our way to get some gold, remember?"

Rhett halted to stare at the Cheyennes, and Hall said, "For *Shelby*, Cap'n. Or did you forget?"

They had all halted, waiting impatiently for him to move on.

"Chrissake, Cap'n!" Hall said. "Let's go before them red bastards change their mind and come at *us*."

"They're still far enough away that we can beat them into the town," Rhett said.

"You lost your goddamn mind?"

Rhett called out, "About face! We're going back!"

There was no movement except for the jostling of the restless horses.

"You heard me!" Rhett shouted.

There were muttered curses, but seven of the men wheeled their mounts. They sat there then, waiting.

"Forward—trot!"

The curses were louder this time, but those facing back rode off. Rhett spurred up past them to the lead.

He rode fifty yards, then looked back over his shoulder. Others were pivoting, and one by one they all fell in, spurring to catch up.

All except Corporal Hall.

Let him go it alone then, Rhett thought. He doesn't know where to dig.

Hall, in turn, glanced back and saw them all riding away. Let the damn fools go, he thought. He knew something none of the others was aware of, including Rhett.

Last night, from his tent alongside Rhett's, he'd heard the captain having some sort of nightmare. It had awakened Hall, and he'd listened to the half-incoherent rambling, first with irritation, then with interest.

At one point Rhett had blurted out something about "the bend in the arroyo" before subsiding into deep sleep.

The phrase had stuck with Hall. He had remembered it this morning, and he had thought about it again after they took to the trail.

He'd just bet those gold bars were somewhere in the bend

of a dry wash. And likely not too far from a wrecked wagon Rhett had earlier told him he'd had to abandon.

It was worth taking a chance on, Corporal Hall thought. He just might hit it lucky. That's how you always found gold—by luck.

Hall was a gambler. He'd take a chance. Just so it wasn't a chance of getting killed trying to defend that damn townful of Yankees.

Lieutenant Eilers and his hardcases, hidden and watching, had been waiting for the former rebel captain and his men to arrive.

Instead, a solitary horseman rode into view. He halted and carefully scanned the terrain around him, and eventually went to the bend in the arroyo and spent a long time studying it. He appeared to come to a decision, and dismounted and picketed his horse. He took a short-handled shovel from its ties behind his saddle. He slid down the bank into the bed of the arroyo and began to dig.

The lieutenant watched him dig for quite a while. Then he came out of his concealment with two of his troopers by his side.

Hall looked up and saw them watching, and the shovel dropped from his hands.

"Go right ahead, Corporal," Eilers said. "Placer mining?"

Hall struggled to speak, and finally said, "Seems a likely place." He stooped and recovered the shovel.

"It does at that. A man knows what he's doing, he might find some sizable nuggets here. You got any reason to believe that's so?"

"None at all, suh."

Eilers studied the corporal's stripes. "One of those Galvanized Yankees, aren't you?"

"Yes, suh."

"Riding escort for the stages?"

"That's right, suh."

"Where's your sergeant and the others?"

"What others, suh?"

"You weren't alone when you left the Springs."

Hall felt sudden anger that he was alone in this predicament. "Damn fools turned back when they saw some Injuns headed toward there."

"That was inconsiderate of them," Eilers said. "To leave you to do all this digging yourself."

"Was my own idea to dig. Heard about a big flood here this last spring. Thought it might have washed something down from the mountains."

"Good thinking, Corporal. I got plenty of men with me, and what we're going to do, we're going to help you dig."

"I don't need no help," Hall said. "What I mean, I don't think there's nothing here after all."

"You may need a lot of help. Hell, you might find some nuggets weigh seventy-five pounds."

Hall's face turned pale. But he was tough. He said, "If we was to hit it lucky, suh, would you give a man his rightly due?"

"Sure, Corporal. You'll get what's coming to you. We're all part of the same army now, aren't we, reb?"

CHAPTER 12

RHETT'S men were riding fast and kicking up dust. Off to their left, and only a short distance behind, the Cheyenne war party was keeping pace.

They're dead set on wiping out the town, Rhett thought. That Dog Soldier leader would not be distracted from his aim, not even by the much smaller force of cavalry.

It was a race now, to see if Rhett and his men could hold their lead and reach the town in time to alert it. All thought of Shelby had left Rhett. His concern, again, was for Sherry.

And, suddenly, he saw a vision of her ahead. She was riding toward him, in split skirt, a hat, held by a thong, blown back to reveal her hair.

And then he knew she was real.

He was afraid to slow because of the Cheyennes, but he was fearful she would ride into them head-on.

Then, relieved, he saw her rein aside, pivot her mount and put it into a trot as she fell in with the squad.

She drew in beside Rhett, her horse picking up the pace to match his.

"What are you doing here?" he said.

"I came to warn you, Justin!"

"Of the Cheyenne back there? How could you know?"

"Cheyenne?" She turned her head to look behind to her left. "Is it Lone Buffalo again?"

"I'm sure of it," he said. "On his way to exact his revenge."

"Oh God!" she said. "Of course I didn't know!"

"Then what—"

"They've laid a trap for you down the trail. That agent, Fenton, let it slip."

His skin prickled. Then they knew. They had known all along. They'd been waiting for him to lead them to the gold, then drop the guillotine. He said, "Colorado Volunteers?"

"I guess. Whoever has been working with Fenton."

He thought of Corporal Hall, and said dully, "If we hadn't turned back, we'd have ridden right into it."

"But you *did* turn back," she said. "To save us. Oh, Justin!"

They thundered toward the town. Rhett drew and fired his revolver when they were two miles away, to alert the citizens. Almost at once he saw them come spilling out of the buildings. A few appeared to have weapons in their hands, expecting the worst. Others were running back inside as if to get theirs.

Rhett threw a glance behind him. The Cheyennes, their mounts more lightly loaded, were closing in. They were only two hundred yards back now, and the yipping braves in the lead let go with a few wild shots.

Beside him, Sherry rode, leaning low, her face white and tense. His glance at her sent fear clutching at him. They had to reach the town before they were cut off. If not, they were all lost—the troopers, the people of Cheyenne Springs. And Sherry.

They hit the outskirts with their lead cut to a hundred yards.

"Dismount and fire!" Rhett yelled.

Two troopers grabbed at dropped reins to hold the horses. The others hit the ground and opened up with carbines on the lead Cheyennes.

From nearby a dozen townsmen joined in with rifle fire.

The Cheyennes broke, retreated to a distance, and went into their familiar riding circle. They left several braves lying in the dust.

Now Lone Buffalo showed himself. Proudly, and bold, he rode at the head of his Dog Soldiers as they made their first encirclement just beyond effective weapons range.

A voice called to Rhett, and he turned and saw Evans running toward him.

The storekeeper arrived, a rifle in his grasp. "Thank God!" he said. "You came back." His eyes swung to Sherry. "Your doing?"

"He was on his way here when I met him."

"We're in for it bad this time," Evans said. "If we hadn't heard your warning shots, we'd be dead now." He paused. "Word from Searle was that you'd deserted the station, Rhett."

Rhett ignored the comment. His eyes were on the Cheyennes as they rode a tightening circle. But his jaw went taut, working the muscles in his neck.

Evans said, "That's Lone Buffalo out there."

"I know."

"You know what that sash he's wearing means?"

Rhett stared at the wide band of buffalo hide, several feet long, that the Dog Soldier chief had thrown over his right shoulder. At the lower end was fastened what looked like a picket pin. Colored porcupine quills ornamented the sash.

Evans said, "They call that a dog rope."

"Dog rope?"

"It means he will never surrender. If he has to, he'll stake himself to the ground and die fighting before he'll quit. He means business this time. No quarter. He'll wipe us out or he'll die here."

"I know that," Rhett said. "Sherry, run for your father's office. We'll be getting casualties soon, and they'll be coming fast."

She touched her fingertips to his shoulder, turned without a word and ran for the street. At that moment a barrage of bullets ripped into the nearest false-fronts from the opposite side of the town.

She ducked back into a gap between the structures. The barrage stopped and she raced out to cross the roadway.

Rhett and Evans stared, held rigid by their fear for her.

Evans said tightly, "I think the world of that girl, Sergeant."

It was nothing that Rhett didn't know. He said, "Get back into your store. On the way, pass the word you'll hand out weapons and ammunition to all who need them. And I hope to hell you're well stocked. You understand?"

The merchant nodded. "I got guns broke out and ready, waiting ever since we survived that last attack, and knew there'd be another coming." He started off.

Rhett halted him. "Are there any good shots among your people? I mean sharpshooters."

"A few, maybe."

"I want them posted on the rooftops."

"Will do," Evans said, and moved off at a run.

Rhett turned to McGregor. "There are wagons on the street. Grab a few civilians and get them moved across the roadway at both ends. Have them stretch ropes between to complete barricades, then stay there in firing positions."

"Yes, suh!" McGregor headed for a nearby cluster of the townsmen who appeared to be arguing among themselves. They broke off their talk and quickly submitted to his relayed orders.

Rhett turned back to his own men. "Split up, half on each side of the street. Take advantage of the cover of the buildings and the sheds where you can. But stay out there on the perimeter where you can keep those Injuns in sight. Don't let any of them get in. We're the army here, we're the first line of defense.

"Stuart, you're in command of that side. Howard, Brogden, Kramer, Ellis, Smith, you're in his detail."

Stuart and his men crossed on the double.

The Cheyennes were within range now, and the shooting on both sides opened up.

Sherry had just reached Craig's office when an arrow came out of nowhere and pinned the sleeve of her blouse to the door.

Rhett, giving her a final quick glance, saw it happen and felt his blood run cold. He could not tell if she was hit. Then she reached across and broke off the shaft. Freed, she slipped inside, and he breathed again.

Her father he had glimpsed on the street, awaiting casualties.

The pair of them would be busy, he thought bitterly, before this day was over. That's if any of them survived the Dog Soldier attack.

And now it began in earnest.

The sun-blasted roofs of the wood structures were like tinder. And a single flaming arrow, shot from the bow of a sacrificing Dog Soldier, caught a corner of a southwestern-most building. In seconds the flames spread to the adjoining one that housed the livery stables.

Cries of "Fire! Fire!" sounded above the rattle of weaponry. Rhett spared a single glance at the leaping flames, his heart sinking. But panicked townsmen closeby stared, stunned, forgetting for a moment the fight itself.

Rhett guessed at once that the fire was a diversion set by Lone Buffalo's orders. He could see that for now the Dog Soldier chief had split his forces into four attack groups, and at once they came driving in from north, south, east, and west, in direct assault.

He shouted his own warning, heard it picked up and relayed, saw the fire ignored now in the greater desperation of trying to repel the horde's attempt to overwhelm.

Ignored even as the screams of horses trapped in the burning stables curdled the blood of those who heard. Ignored, too, as a rifleman posted on a third burning roof leaped when his clothes caught fire.

He struck the ground feet first, and a leg twisted under him; he shrieked his pain as a bone snapped on impact.

The Cheyennes came on and on in the face of the defenders' withering barrage. Their own shots from jostling horseback were surprisingly effective, judged by the scattered cries of townsmen taking hits.

They thundered in to the perimeter's edge, and only then did the wave subside as their weapons ran empty and they sought to reload on plunging mounts. The townsmen, better armed, took several Dog Soldiers in decimating fire. Some turned and fled. But other braves overrode the defense positions and boiled into the street. The defenders turned and caught them as they tried to reload.

At the west end, where the fire still blazed, the Indians had reached the barricades, killed the defenders, and slashed through the strung ropes. They came tearing down the roadway toward the others.

They fired as they came, into the structures and every visible target that took their eyes. They reached the middle of the town before they ran out of ammunition.

They yelled and struck out, using empty weapons as clubs. They drove their ponies into and over the dismounted townsmen.

The Galvanized Yankees under Stuart charged in toward the street and shot them off their horses. Trooper Kramer said to Stuart, "They got to be the craziest, gutsiest fighters I ever seen."

"Stay down!" Stuart yelled, just as a bullet shattered a window next to where they crouched. He caught the movement of a Cheyenne lying prone in the dust and put a bullet into his skull. "Like somebody said awhile back, a dead Injun ain't always a good Injun," he said.

"I believe it now," Kramer said.

From up on a roof, one of the posted riflemen fired and another fallen brave jerked nearly upright, then fell face down, showing the back of his head blown out as his bonnet headband split. Beside him the pile of released crow feathers formed the grisly look of a feasting buzzard.

The nearest civilian defenders had joined Stuart's men in mopping up the fallen Cheyenne.

Among them was Oakley Simpson, the town blacksmith, a heavy-muscled man who had just fired his last bullet into the heart of a still-breathing Cheyenne. Some instinct caused him to whirl just as another leaped toward him from behind, a tomahawk in hand.

Oakley caught the descending wrist, pivoted and threw the brave over his shoulder, letting him fly loose to land, stunned, several feet away.

He rushed after him. The brave gained his feet, but his head hung low, his long black hair dangling loose.

The blacksmith grabbed the full head of hair in his powerful hands, pivoted again, and repeated the shoulder throw.

The brave was big and heavy, and halfway through the throw, at the point of maximum stress, he screamed. Screamed as his scalp tore loose from his skull and his whole head blossomed red like a huge flower bursting into bloom.

He fell into the dirt, writhing and shrieking his agony, and Simpson rushed over and stomped him to death as if he were killing a bug.

A shift of the wind halted the spread of the fire, but smoke from it had partly obscured the town. Rhett strained his eyes to make out the Cheyennes who had retreated; they were now regrouping north of the town. He guessed they'd lost half their fighting men in Lone Buffalo's fanatical attacks.

And it was the reb troopers who had inflicted most of the losses. The years of combat against the North had paid off here—ironically—in thus far saving the northern sympathizers.

But he knew the Dog Soldier leader, wearing that sash they called the dog rope, would never give up. There would be no enduring respite for the town. Not as long as Lone Buffalo lived.

And now they came again, a regrouped force of those he had been watching through the haze. They came charging toward that part of the defense he held with his half dozen troopers.

There were four times that number racing toward him.

At that moment Stuart came sprinting across the street, his half of the rebs behind him. "No attack on our side!" he cried.

The combined squad opened fire on the charging Dog Soldiers.

Evans, too, was suddenly with Rhett, and shooting. "No more guns to give out," he said, and fired again.

At that, the attackers almost overwhelmed them. They got so close that Rhett, his carbine emptied, dropped it, drew his revolver, and emptied that too before the wave of warriors was halted.

At that point Evans cried out and fell back, an arrow jutting from beneath his arm.

He pulled himself to his knees and stayed there, rigid with pain. His face was pale, and blood stained his shirt in a small red ring around the arrow shaft.

The Cheyennes had turned and were riding hard to get out of range of the troopers' weapons. Again they left many dead behind them.

Rhett turned to the storekeeper and said, "Let me look at that." He shoved his revolver into his holster.

Evans stood up. He staggered a little but stayed on his feet. "No," he said. He looked shocked, but his speech was clear. "No. Not you. I'll go over and get Sherry to do it."

"She and Craig have wounded waiting."

"I'll take my turn," Evans said. Before Rhett could stop him, he started across the roadway.

He's not thinking clear, Rhett thought. But he could waste no more time on the storekeeper. He picked up his emptied carbine and shoved cartridges into the butt-stock magazine tube. He was just in time, as a suicidal handful of young braves suddenly reversed direction and charged still again.

The light attack was beaten back at once. And when he

looked again for Evans, he was across the road and stagger-
ing up toward Craig's place.

Sherry suddenly ran out of the office and rushed to help
him. But she never got there.

From behind a structure two doors down, a Dog Soldier
raced into the street, saw her, pivoted his horse and swept
her up and across its withers, and disappeared between
buildings down the way.

Rhett had his carbine raised, but feared to shoot because
of Sherry.

"Sergeant!" Evans yelled. "That's Lone Buffalo!"

Rhett's horse was at a rack nearby. He reached it at a run,
tore loose the reins and leaped into the saddle, but dropped
his carbine.

He spurred past Evans, almost knocking him down, and
plunged into the passage the Cheyenne had taken.

Lone Buffalo headed south, straight for the river.

Rhett could see Sherry kicking and thrashing, trying to
slip off the horse. The Cheyenne leader kicked his pony into
a run to prevent it.

What the hell had driven the man into town alone? Rhett
wondered.

It came to him then. *Vengeance.* With his repeated attacks
beaten off by the defenders, Lone Buffalo had come to seek
his revenge on a personal level.

He was looking for me, Rhett thought. One way or another
the brave, proud, vengeful son of a bitch would have satisfaction from the man he believed had betrayed his kin.

The white woman on the street had been no more than a
target of opportunity for him, Rhett thought. He had seen
Rhett and impulsively grabbed her as bait to lead Rhett out.

Out to a solitary fate.

Lone Buffalo wanted Rhett alone.

Rhett drove in his spurs. He'd give him what he wanted.

Fenton had been firing from the opened window of his

hotel room, the same window from which he had killed the
half-breed and brought on this retribution. It was as good a
position as any, and better than some, he thought. There
were disadvantages, though. His vision to either side was
limited, and of course he had no sight at all of what was
going on behind him.

As the handful of young Cheyennes drove in on Rhett's
position, Fenton was aware that Rhett was there. He had
seen him tear into town just ahead of the attackers, and was
at first upset. He wanted the reb captain down there leading
Eilers to the gold. By now, his feelings had changed somewhat. He realized that the town—and his own life, most
probably—had survived this far because of the fighting
ability of the Galvanized rebels.

He was now equally concerned with Rhett's own survival.
The man was the key to the gold. He damned sure didn't
want him killed, not when the scheme was so close to fulfill-
ment. Goddammit! It couldn't happen now. He took pride
in what he did for the Secret Service and Allan Pinkerton.
He could not let the plan fail.

His urge to help Rhett repulse the charge made him lean
out the window for better aim. Too late he saw the warrior
holding the bow from which discharged an arrow.

It drove deep into his chest. He dropped the Henry rifle
as he fell backward into the room.

He got to his feet, turned toward the door and began
walking. He walked slowly down the stairs to the lobby. It
was empty. The clerk was outside defending the town like
everybody else.

He went out and looked across and over to Doc Craig's
place. He got down the portico steps without falling and
walked out into the street. He kept walking toward the
doctor's office, although the wound in his chest was causing
him to slow.

Some of the lesser wounded were huddled about the

front. One of them looked up, his own pain showing. His eyes widened, and he said, "Christ! Here's another took an arrow."

Craig was in his doorway, appearing distraught. He kept saying, "What happened to Sherry? Somebody tell me what happened to Sherry."

Evans was sitting on the stoop in front of the door. He said, "That Dog Soldier chief grabbed her and rode off."

"Get her back!" Craig cried. "Dammit! Somebody get her back!"

"The reb captain went," Evans said. "He was right on their heels."

"Him!" Craig said.

"Best damned man you'll ever see," Evans said. His eyes suddenly were caught by Fenton, who stood swaying on his feet. "Doc, that man's bad hurt."

Even as he spoke, Fenton pitched face forward on the ground. They could hear the arrow shaft snap as he fell on it.

The professionalism in Doc Craig took over. In quick strides he reached Fenton's side, and bent over him.

A man limping with a leg wound went to aid him.

"Help me get him inside," Craig said. And over his shoulder, "You'd best come in, too, Jed."

"I don't need any favored treatment," Evans said.

"Come in, I said."

The limping casualty helped get Fenton on an oilcloth-covered table. "You don't mind, Doc, I'll wait outside. I got a weak stomach when it comes to seeing arrows pulled."

Craig did not answer. He was giving Evans a cursory examination. "Damned thing is imbedded in your trapezius muscle," he said. "Sit down, Jed. I'll get to you when I can."

"It hurts like hell."

"No doubt," Craig said. He was already studying Fenton, lying on the table.

So far, Fenton hadn't said a word.

"It get his lung, Doc?" Evans said.

"Probably."

Fenton muttered suddenly, "Then I don't have a chance."

"You don't know that," Craig said.

"*You* do."

Craig did not reply.

Fenton said, "It's so, isn't it?"

"I can't tell yet," Craig said.

"Don't try to pull the arrow out, Doc. The pain won't be worth it. I'm dying and I know it."

Craig kept looking at the wound, trying to make up his mind.

"I've bought it," Fenton rasped. "That I know. And I got something on my chest besides an arrow."

"I'm not a priest."

"Don't matter. I'm not a Catholic." He coughed, and blood showed on his lips. He said, "I did a despicable thing." His voice was weaker now. "I started it around that Rhett once stirred up Injuns to kill whites. I lied. There's no evidence he ever did that."

His voice dropped so low that Craig leaned over him to listen.

Evans pulled himself to his feet and came over, clutching at Craig's shoulder to stay erect, but wanting to hear.

"The reb is innocent," Fenton said, his voice abruptly loud, then breaking as he had another fit of coughing.

"How do you know all that?" Craig said.

"Secret Service. I'm Secret Service," Fenton said. "Tell him to watch out. There's a trap set for him. You hear?"

"A trap?"

"By Lieutenant Eilers—Sand Creek soldiers." Fenton's head rolled to one side then and stayed.

"You hear all that?" Craig asked.

"I heard," Evans said. "A trap for Rhett, Doc. The man who went off to save your daughter."

"Sherry!" Craig cried. It was as if he'd forgotten about her momentarily. "I've got to know what happened!"

Rhett gained on the Indian pony.

And then, abruptly, the Cheyenne plunged into the fringe of trees that lined the river, splashed across a shallow current, and reined up on a barren sandbar. He pivoted his horse to face Rhett and let Sherry slip to the ground.

His eyes went to Rhett's saddle scabbard and noted his missing carbine. A faint smile touched his lips. He held a long war lance.

Rhett flipped open his holster as he reached him, jerked free his Colt and cocked it.

The Cheyenne lost his smile.

"Drop the lance!" Rhett said. "I owe you that."

Instead, Lone Buffalo kicked his pony's flanks and rushed him, lance leveled at his guts.

Rhett pulled the trigger, and remembered too late that the gun was empty, empty from repulsing the attack that had wounded Evans. He threw himself far to one side, kicking loose from his off stirrup.

The lance missed him by an inch, but the pony struck his horse as it went past, knocking him from the saddle. He barely got his left foot free.

He landed hard in the sand and scrambled to his feet. He still had his saber, and he drew it.

The Cheyenne wheeled and came at him again, the pony's hooves threshing at the sand. Rhett stepped aside and swung the blade, but awkwardly, in a backhand. The tip drew a gash across the Cheyenne's bare calf and blood spurted from it.

The Indian realized the pony could not maneuver in the sand. He slid off its back and faced Rhett, lance held at the ready.

Sherry stood to one side, her face drawn in terror.

The Cheyenne moved in, thrusting with his lance.

Rhett slashed at it, heard the blade ring against the iron

tip as he parried it aside. He slipped along the length of the lance, slashed again, and felt a jolt as the saber rebounded from the iron-hard hickory shaft.

The Cheyenne stepped back two quick paces, then thrust the lance again, using both hands to drive it.

Rhett parried it to his left, stepped in and grabbed the shaft in his left hand and jerked himself forward. He pumped his feet into the sand, driving himself within saber reach.

There was no panic on Lone Buffalo's face.

Rhett did not slash again. He thrust the saber straight forward, but was overbalanced and tripped.

The Cheyenne tried to leap backward but failed.

The saber point drove in under the breastbone, and Rhett felt it strike bone-deep in the man's back. He let go of the haft as the weight of the Cheyenne's body twisted it from his hand.

Sherry struggled forward and threw her arms around him.

He was sick, and he thrust her away.

She looked hurt, and he saw that, and he said, "I'm sorry. But he helped me when I needed help bad. I owed him a debt, not a death."

He lifted her up behind his saddle, and swung up himself. He did not speak again as they rode hard back into town. She was silent too, knowing he was sickened by his duel to the death with a man who had done him a great favor.

But she clung to him tightly.

He had let the Indian pony go, hoping it would return to the other Cheyennes, alerting them that they no longer had a leader.

He halted at Craig's office, his face blank as he saw Craig come out. Sherry slid down and stumbled into her father's arms.

Craig looked up at Rhett and said, "No way I can repay you for what you've done."

Rhett turned away, still silent. He rode to where he could

watch the Cheyenne warriors still gathered in the distance. There was some movement among them now.

Another attack? he wondered. Or were they discouraged by the casualties they had suffered? To trade heavy losses for an objective was not an Indian way, he knew. They were mostly hit-and-run fighters.

In that, they had more sense than white men, he thought, recalling the sacrificial battles between the North and the South.

He saw a single brave ride up from the river toward them, the body of another slung across a pony led behind. It could be Lone Buffalo's corpse. Might it be that the Cheyenne rider had witnessed the duel from hiding?

He dismounted and went to where his men were waiting and watching too.

There was agitation out there as the Indian brought in the corpse and presented it to the other warriors.

"Do you think—" McGregor said, then broke off as the whole warrior bunch began to ride away. They rode slowly, seemingly with reluctance on the part of some. Then even these stragglers fell in and followed.

"That looks like the end, suh," McGregor said.

The words did not touch Rhett. He had his mind on other problems he had to resolve now. Mostly with Sherry.

Craig, having cleaned and bandaged Evans's wound, released him to pass the word of Fenton's confession. It was the least he could do to repay the rescue of his daughter.

Evans, though weakened and hurting, was eager, too, to do this. He had never been convinced the rumor about Rhett was true. He had heard a lot of rumors during his career as a storekeeper, and he had learned to discount at least half of what he heard.

His first contact was with Rhett himself.

Rhett immediately had questions. "This trap—who did he say was in command of it?"

"A Lieutenant Eilers, I think he said. With a bunch of Sand Creek soldiers."

"*Lieutenant* Eilers?"

"You know him?"

"I met him once. When he was a sergeant at Fort Lyon."

"Why would they set a trap for you?"

Rhett shrugged and said nothing.

Evans eyed him speculatively, then said, "Well, you're warned." He paused. "Sherry is waiting for you."

She was already back helping her father care for the other wounded.

None of them were Rhett's men. Pure luck had spared them. Four of the troopers had minor flesh wounds that were being treated by their comrades.

But there was nothing serious enough to delay his mission.

The quick about-face in attitude of the citizens, which he was now sensing, as they realized he had saved them from being massacred—it irritated rather than pleased him. How fickle they were, he thought. How quickly they could be turned around.

Well, by God, he couldn't! He was going after that gold and taking it to Shelby. He'd let nothing stop him now. Nothing.

And then she came running out as he dismounted in front of Craig's.

In her embrace, his determination wavered.

"Justin," she said, "I love you so!"

It was a moment before he could speak. "Sherry," he said then, "I've got to finish what I started out to do."

"What do you mean?"

"I have a mission to complete—for the South."

"For the South? But the war is over."

"My mission isn't."

"What mission?"

"I can't tell you that, Sherry. Even you."

She drew back to study his face. "But how long will it take?"

"Years, maybe."

"Years!" she said. "Years, Justin?"

He could feel her trembling, as if with fright. "I'm sorry," he said.

"Sorry? You're *sorry?* Is that all you feel?" She pulled away from him.

He said slowly, "No. No, I feel a lot more than that. I do love you, Sherry. Believe that."

"No, I won't believe it. Not if you're going to leave me. For years? Do you expect me to wait years for you?"

He was suddenly angered and said, cruelly, "You'll always have your husband's ghost to keep you warm."

"What a thing to say!"

He felt instant remorse. "Yes. I should never have said that."

"You'll ride south again," she said. "You'll ride to your first love, the South. It means more to you than I."

"It's not the same."

"No, it's stronger." There was a resignation in her voice. "The South has a hold on you I can never match."

It must be true, he thought. If it wasn't, he would not be leaving.

"I'm sorry," he said again.

She stumbled away, then turned as she reached her father's doorway. He could see she was crying. It made him feel like crying too.

She said, "I'll always love you, Justin. Remember that." And she was gone.

CHAPTER 13

AT the cache site, the hardcase troopers under Lieutenant Eilers were digging, along with Corporal Hall—and finding nothing.

Eilers called a halt to the excavating.

"It appears you don't know any more than we do," he said.

"I didn't say I did."

"Too bad. If your Johnny Reb comrades survive that Cheyenne attack, they'll be coming back for sure. And we'll be waiting for them. Now we can't leave you free to maybe warn them, can we?"

"I'll join your outfit," Hall said desperately.

"No," Eilers said. "You just keep standing in that hole you're digging. It'll make it easier to bury you." He reached for his flap holster and drew his army Colt.

At that moment one of his men let out a yell. He dropped his shovel, fell to his knees, and began throwing handfuls of sand to either side.

They all turned to look at him. And stared in fascination as he tugged loose an ingot of shining gold.

Hall knew there was no hope for him now. He scrambled out of the hole, his shovel in his hand. He took a fast step toward the lieutenant, whose face was turned, and swung the shovel blade at his head.

The crunch of his boots against some gravel made Eilers whirl. He ducked, and the wide swing of the shovel carried Hall around, and Eilers shot him in the back. Then he shot him in the head.

The others barely glanced up at what was going on. Their attention went immediately back to the ingot.

And then, with wild fury, they attacked the sand.

Two days later Rhett again led his men down the Fort Lyon Trail. He had been delayed while the minor wounds received by four of them healed enough that they could ride. This time it was McGregor who rode beside him. McGregor said, "Cap'n, we heard what Miz Cowper said when she rode down to warn us. We all know now that we was riding into an ambush if we hadn't turned around. You reckon it'll be the same now?"

Rhett said, "At least we won't be taken by surprise."

"Somebody besides us must know about the gold."

"Somebody does," Rhett said.

"If it's gone?"

"If it's gone, we'll find it."

"Cap'n, where do you think General Jo Shelby is now?"

"He'll be in Mexico, most likely. I waited too long."

"You had your reasons, Cap'n." McGregor smiled. "Not the least was that doctor lady. I was some in love with her myself."

Rhett gave him a quick look. But he didn't take Mac's words seriously.

"She was so beautiful and kind," the trooper said. "Don't think I'll ever forget her."

"Enough of that!" Rhett said.

McGregor looked at him, saw the pain in Rhett's face, and said, "Begging the captain's pardon, suh!"

"It's all right, Mac. Forget it."

They rode in silence for a few moments before McGregor spoke again. "Suh, is it right to call you Cap'n now?"

The thought struck Rhett then that for the job he had to do, he could tolerate no dissent in his command. There could be no more borderline insubordination such as he had allowed Corporal Hall for old time's sake. They were going back to war.

He said, "Yes."

"The men have been thinking on it, Cap'n, now that they feel like southerners again. They'll be glad to hear."

Their approach had been cautious, and Rhett scrutinized, then scouted thoroughly, the surrounding *malpaís* before he led his squad to where the charred remains of his wagon lay. There was evidence—prints and scuffed earth—that a body of men had been busy here.

They could see the holes in the arroyo sand where the ingots had been uncovered.

The holes had been left unfilled. All except the one in which the stiffened corpse of Corporal Hall slumped waist-deep. His upper body had fallen over, face down in the sand, exposing the wound that had shattered his spine and the one that had blown out the back of his head.

"Lord God!" McGregor said. "Who did that to him?"

"Bluebellies," Rhett said.

Behind him, Private Brogden said, "Christ!"

There was controlled rage in Rhett's voice when he spoke. "All of you men take a good look at him. And remember what you've seen. You're wearing the blue, and that may help us where we're going. But from this day onward, underneath you are wearing the gray."

"Aye to that, Cap'n," Brogden said.

They carried Corporal Hall up out of the arroyo and dug him a proper grave, and then they searched about until they found the tracks left by those who had killed him.

The trail went southeasterly.

They're skirting the fort, Rhett thought. Just as I would have done last year.

That told him something about the bastards who had done Hall in. From what he had learned from Sherry, they were supposed to be working for the War Department. If they were avoiding contact with the fort, that cast considerable doubt on their loyalty.

With Eilers, now a lieutenant, commanding a detachment of Sand Creek killers, a picture was beginning to fall into place.

McGregor said, "They've got some lead on us, suh."

"We're traveling lighter, Mac. They're carrying a ton of gold."

"Must be big as a mountain."

"Matter of fact those seventy-five-pound bars are pretty small. Gold weighs about two and a half times heavy as iron. You can slip one of those bars into a saddlebag easy enough, and have room left over."

"How many men you figure they got, Cap'n?"

"By their tracks, I'd guess maybe twenty."

"Those are heavy odds, suh. Especially now with Corporal Hall gone."

"We'll find a way to cut those odds."

"We've got field rations for a week, suh. Beyond that we'll be foraging?"

"Whatever it takes, Mac."

After a moment, McGregor said, "Those bluebellies, are they deserters?"

"If they pass Fort Lyon, we can guess they are."

"I reckon that now we're deserters too," Mac said.

"That was our intention."

"Yes, suh. Still, it bothers me somewhat."

Rhett was silent. It bothered him, too. It was one more thing he had to put from his mind. He had to concentrate on completing his mission, no matter what.

Lieutenant Eilers was a man in a hurry now. He knew he was a wanted man, and his one idea was to reach Mexico, where he would not be endangered by either Union or Confederate forces. He expected to find some of the latter present still in Texas, and wanted to hold his men together for the protection of himself.

They were a mutinous bunch, he thought. It had taken much persuasion on his part to keep several of them from heading toward Santa Fe when they crossed the Trail.

One of them, who he knew had cut out the genitals of a squaw for a souvenir at Sand Creek, was as intractable as a bull. His name was Sykes, and he was of a mind to take his share of the gold to California.

Lieutenant Eilers wished he could have brought men of his old command, men of the 1st Colorado, instead of these castoffs of the Bloody 3rd.

There were some good, courageous men in the 1st. And, of course, in the 2nd, which had fought the Confederates in Missouri. But you couldn't get *good* men to do what he wanted them to do. Which was to steal the gold from the government.

Well, once he reached Mexico he'd pick the most tractable of the bunch, and they'd eliminate the others. Then he'd settle down and live like one of those rich *hacendados*—he and the chosen few he selected for mutual protection against the Mexes.

Eilers didn't think the Mexicans would be much of a problem. He didn't hold them in high regard, those he'd had contact with.

Sykes pulled up alongside him and interrupted his thoughts. "I still say we could have done better in California, damn it!"

"The United States Government has got a long arm," Eilers said. "And they've got a roster of our names."

"You think they can't reach us in Mexico?"

"Down there we'll be safe."

"You better be right, by God!"

"I'll not take any more of your insubordination, Sykes."

Sykes laughed. "Hell, you ain't a army officer no more. You're a outlaw just like the rest of us."

"I'm still in command here."

"Excuse *me*, Lieutenant, sir!" Sykes said.

Eilers gave him a bitter glance. The muscles in his jaw worked. For the first time since he had avoided Fort Lyon, he was aware that he had lost the authority he'd carried for several years, the clout given him by virtue of his sergeant's stripes and, more lately, his officer's bars.

He was used to giving orders and tolerating no disobedience. The knowledge that he could not command so strongly by force of personality alone was intolerable to him. For a moment he regretted his trade-off. Then, slowly, the thought of his easy future in Mexico erased the regret.

His rage, though, at Sykes's insubordination did not leave him. Sykes would be the first to die, when his usefulness was over.

They were in Comanche country now, homeland of the Kwahadi band, and Eilers, uneasily aware of this, veered easterly. He had fought the Comanche along the Santa Fe Trail a time or two, and he had a dread of doing it again, especially because of the precious cargo he was carrying.

He crossed the Canadian River and the headwaters of the Red, then the Pease, and struck out for the Brazos, whereon he had heard rumors that scattered pioneer ranchers had built a few stockades west of old Fort Belknap. These they garrisoned themselves, precariously—and sometimes disastrously, when raided.

He might raid there himself, he thought. There might be some provisions stored there to replenish his own depleted supplies.

Although he was not certain he was being followed, he knew there was that possibility. It had decided him to keep moving, wasting no time looking for game. They had seen no buffalo.

Nor ranches, not even abandoned ones.

He was still west of the Texas frontier, and he was driven ever further east, searching for it.

Gradually the deserted vestiges of it appeared: a shack here, a corral there, skeletons of livestock. A hundred miles of this until finally, by sheer luck, they blundered upon Fort Murrah, near where Elm Creek poured into the Brazos.

Murrah was a small crude monument to the courage of those Texas settlers who had stubbornly remained, drawing a line from which they would not retreat. Thus far had the Texas frontier retreated, and no farther, even in the face of increased Comanche boldness when the Indians realized the west Texas defenses had crumbled while the white men fought a great war among themselves.

Fort Murrah was a square log stockade with picket bastions. A meager refuge for those in the area who could reach it in times of raid.

Old Fort Belknap was somewhere to the east, and God only knew who was garrisoning it now, Eilers thought. He'd heard it had been manned by Texas militia during the war, but now federal troops could have taken over. Either way, he had reason to stay clear of both forces.

Eilers halted his men in some creek foliage while he reconnoitered. The little stockade appeared to be deserted. There was no noise from within. But a lone saddle mount was picketed, grazing, a short distance from its gate.

Eilers moved in quickly then. He discovered a rope-activated bell on the gate and rang it.

After a bit, a man's voice from within challenged him. "State your business and who you are!"

Eilers was certain there was a peephole somewhere in the log gate from which he was being scrutinized. Clad in Union blue, he made the best of it.

"Lieutenant Eilers, and a detachment of federal cavalry. Open up!"

There was a long hesitation.

"You heard the order!" Eilers said. "Do you want us to bust down this gate?"

He immediately heard a bolt being slid. His men had rejoined him, and he motioned them to push the gate inward. They swung it open.

An elderly man in work garb stood facing them. There was a scowl on his face. He said, "Lieutenant, this here is a private-built fort. Not built by the state of Texas, and damned sure not built by you goddamned Yankees."

"The war is over, old man," Eilers said. "Texas is beaten, or haven't you heard?"

"I heard," the old man said. He hesitated, then said, "What you want with us?"

"Food and quarters for the night. And provisions to go."

The old man seemed relieved, but he still scowled. "Go where?"

"None of your business. I've been told you Texans know better than to ask questions like that."

The old Texan nodded. "Reckon so. But sometimes we forget."

"Anybody here but you?"

"Might be."

"Answer my question, dammit!"

"Only me, suh."

"That's better. Rustle us up some grub."

"I ain't no cook, Lieutenant."

"I didn't ask you to cook. You get the grub. We'll do our own cooking."

"I'll show you where the stores are. But we ain't got a hell of a lot. We just keep enough on hand for if the Comanch get to acting up."

"That happen often?"

"They played hell with us last October," the old Texan said. "Hundreds of the bastards—Comanch, and Kiowas too—come swarming into these parts." He paused. "They left us pretty much alone here in the stockade after we shot a few at long range. But they did a share of killing and mutilating, burning and kidnapping of folks that didn't make it back in time. It went on till somebody hit and killed the war chief in charge. They quit then, like they do sometimes, but I reckon you've heard of that before." He stared at Eilers's uniform. "Or have you ever fought Injuns? Maybe fighting and killing southern boys was more your style."

"We're Colorado Territorials," Eilers said. "Out of Fort Lyon. Been fighting Injuns for four years."

The Texan seemed to relent a little. "That's different," he said. "But what the hell you doing in Texas?"

Eilers gave him a long, fixed stare until he fidgeted.

"I keep forgetting," the old man said.

"Get on with what I told you."

The old man moved off toward the storeroom. Eilers followed with a couple of his men.

"How far is it to Fort Belknap?"

"Only a few miles," the caretaker said.

"Any soldiers there?"

"Sure. A platoon of Yankees."

"They do you any good when the Comanches struck?"

"They wasn't here then." The old man's voice turned bitter. "They wouldn't be there now if Lee hadn't surrendered."

"You don't sound glad to have their protection."

"We had our own protection, such as it was. Texas militia was in garrison then."

"And how much good did your Texas militia do you in the big raid?"

"Done as good as them damned bluebellies would, I reckon, except they wasn't enough of them. Most was out hunting Injuns. Was only a lieutenant and fourteen troopers left, and they come running to help when they heard the fracas. Fifteen men and they run smack dab into a couple hundred Comanch and Kiowa, and only half got through to us. Wasn't for them, though, we'd likely not held the Injuns off."

"With a platoon of Federals now," Eilers said, "you got less to worry about."

"I don't cotton to them much more than I do a Comanch," the old man said. "Arrogant bastards, now that Lee surrendered."

"You don't sound pleased the war is over."

"I ain't, goddammit! If they'd left it to us Texans, we'd be fighting yet." The old man turned suddenly on Eilers and said, "Say! You being bluebellies, why in hell don't you ride on to Belknap to draw provisions? Why pick on us?"

"We've got our reason."

"It ain't reason enough!" the old man said, defiant. "You goddamned Yankees think you own Texas now."

"We do. Open up those stores."

The old man stood there, not moving, even though there was no lock on the storeroom door. "I ain't going to do it."

"*Open that door!*"

The old man looked pugnacious. "Over my dead body!" he said.

"I can arrange that," Lieutenant Eilers said. He took his revolver from his holster and shoved it into the old man's ribs. "Do it!"

"Nope."

"*Do it!*"

"I ain't agoing to," the old man said. "Go ahead and shoot."

Eilers let go with a string of curses. He grabbed the old man with his free hand, jerked him aside, and opened the door himself.

The two hardcase soldiers with him stared, then exchanged glances.

"Go on!" Eilers snarled at them. "See what they got in there."

The two men went in. One came back to the door and said, "They got grub, all right."

"Fetch some of it out," Eilers said, and turned to the old Texan standing there glowering at him. He put his revolver back in his holster.

One of the men came out with a sack of foodstuff, and stopped. "Whyn't you shoot the old bastard, Lieutenant?"

"I should have," Eilers said. "But I couldn't. He reminds me too much of my old man."

CHAPTER 14

RHETT followed Eilers's tracks to where they reached the Brazos.

He crossed with his rebels then, but lost the trail on the other side in a maze of hundreds of prints, most of them months old and almost erased by the weather. They had to have been made by Indians, he thought. There weren't enough whites in frontier Texas to leave that many tracks.

They soon spotted the log stockade.

"Well, Cap'n?" McGregor said.

"Stay here under cover," Rhett said. "I'll ride up alone."

"Those bluebellies could be inside waiting, suh."

"I'm thinking of that. I intend to ride a circle around the place, look for their tracks leading out, Sergeant."

"*Sergeant,* suh?"

"As of now," Rhett said. He turned to the others waiting around them. "McGregor will be in command if something happens to me. With the rank of sergeant. Understood?"

There were a few nods, and no comments. Always a ticklish moment when you advanced one man over others, he thought. But it had to be that way. It was the way an army was run.

He turned back to McGregor. "Sergeant, if you must assume command, your orders are to keep on to Mexico and report to General Shelby. With the gold, if you can get it."

"I understand, suh."

Rhett rode slowly around the stockade area, keeping far enough away to be hid. On the south part of his circle he encountered the trail sign of which he had now become familiar.

He turned and rode directly for his men. He signaled them to rejoin him, and together they approached the fort.

As they neared it, the gate swung open enough for the old man to appear.

The old man looked them over, then said, "More of the same, I reckon."

"Open the gate wide," Rhett said. "Who's inside?"

The old man swung it open fully. "Nobody. They done left yesterday morning."

"Who did?"

"Them other Yankee cavalry. Who else?"

Rhett said, "You sound Texan to me."

"I am Texan, goddammit! And I got a bellyful of you thieving Yankee bluecoats as took most of our stores." The old man stopped abruptly. "You got the sound of Texas in your talk yourself. How come you wearing blue?"

"Been Galvanized."

"You *what*?"

"We were Galvanized Yankees."

"I heard some tell they was such a thing," the old man said. "But I never seen one before."

"Once again, I'm Captain Rhett, Confederate States Army."

"Glory be!" the old man said. "You mean we are carrying on?"

"Some of us," Rhett said.

"Best news I've heard since they fired on Fort Sumter!"

"Move back. I'm coming in to inspect."

The old man stepped aside and stood at attention. "Ain't nobody here, suh. You got my word for it."

They tied up their horses to a rack outside and entered.

The old man smiled. "Confederate cavalry, by God! Only thing missing is the right uniform. But you are best off wearing what you got, conditions being what they are."

"Seems most likely," Rhett said.

"I guess you boys will be hungry, though them *real* Yankees took most of what we had here."

"They say what outfit they were?"

"Colorado Territorials. A lieutenant and twenty-odd men. You know him, Cap'n?"

"I know him."

"Friends?"

"Not hardly."

"I'm right glad to hear that. Kind of an ornery bastard, he was. But he had some with him appeared worse."

"They'd be from the Bloody Third."

"Bloody Third?"

"The bunch that killed those friendly Cheyenne women and children at Sand Creek."

"By God! We got news of that. It was played up big in the San Antone newspaper, I heard. Told what murderers them Yankees are!"

"Well, all Yankees aren't like that. Not most Colorado Territorials, either."

"You got business with them, suh?"

"On their trail."

"You got a grievance?"

"You might say that," Rhett said.

"I wish I was going along to see it. But you got plenty of risks ahead of you, suh. Texas is already filling up with bluebelly soldiers—no offense meant for what you're wearing. Then there is what they call the 'bush' soldiers, suh, living however they can—deserters from both armies, and ex-guerrillas armed to the teeth."

"We're not new to fighting," Rhett said.

The old man looked again at the rebel troopers and smiled. "I can see that, suh. I surely can. And now let's see can I find something left in the way of provisions."

They cooked a meal while the old man kept giving Rhett

details of information that had come to him about conditions now prevailing in the state.

"What about Shelby?" Rhett said.

"He got across in time. Fourth of July, to be exact."

"Got across?"

"Crossed the Rio Grande into Mexico from Eagle Pass. With seven hundred troops, I heard."

"Only *seven hundred!*" Rhett said. "Only seven hundred, out of his Iron Brigade?"

"Was a lot of soldiers got tired of waiting once they got back to Texas, I reckon. Or plumb tired of the war." The old man studied Rhett's face. "You was expecting Shelby to hang onto more?"

"I was that."

"Been others crossed to join him since then, I heard. Thousands, maybe. Several generals too, some with Shelby, some later. But they all look to him as leader, even them that outranked him. He's the only one that refused to surrender."

"I hoped to find him before he crossed. The word was he intended to fight on."

"Reckon he will," the old man said. "But it'll be from the other side of the border now."

"That'll have to do," Rhett said.

"If I wasn't so damned old, I'd go with you."

"Well it's a young man's game."

"Ain't it always been?" the old man said.

They moved on, short-rationed, but carrying enough for a week's bare subsistence. They rode echoing the old man's curses against "them *real* bluebellies that stole most of our stores."

Rhett figured they were less than two days behind Eilers now.

McGregor said, "We gaining on them, Cap'n?"

"We're holding our own, at least."

"Is that good enough, suh?"

Rhett had been thinking about this, and now he said, "It just may be. Listening to the old man gave me a new sight on the situation."

"How's that, suh?"

"Looks like we got a gauntlet to run through three hundred miles of Texas to get to Eagle Pass and pick up Shelby's trail. We don't know where Eilers is headed exactly, but I'm guessing it's Mexico too."

"And, suh?"

"They've got us outgunned, with twenty-odd men to protect the gold, and they're carrying for us. And they'll not be mistaken for Confederates. So they've got a better chance of getting through. Might be best to just trail them and hit them on the other side of the border."

"I see, suh," McGregor said. "But what if they're stopped by somebody that finds what they're toting?"

"That could make a difference," Rhett said. "We'll ride faster until we get closer. We've got to see that doesn't happen."

Sergeant McGregor rode in silence for some moments. Then he said, "Hell, suh, we might end up fighting *for* them, to keep that from happening."

"We just might," Rhett said tightly.

"I wouldn't like that, suh. Nor any of the men, I'm sure. Not after what they done to Corporal Hall."

"I wouldn't either," Rhett said. "But we've got to keep our eye on the objective, to get that gold to General Shelby."

He increased the gait. The distance between the Yankee deserters and the rebels grew shorter.

The Kwahadies watched Eilers and his troopers come.

"They are too many," the older, lead Comanche said.

They had seen the pony soldiers for some time, and had waited in hiding in a roll of the grassy plain.

There were only sixteen of them in the party, and the

leader was looking for easier game. "We will let them pass," he said.

There was some grumbling among the younger ones. They had been impatient for action for several days.

"More bluebelly soldiers than we have seen for a long time," another older one said. "Why?"

"The war between the whites is over," the leader said. "Now they come back to fight us again."

"Then we better kill those we can."

Eilers's men went by, unaware.

"They were too many," the leader said again. "We will find others." His keen eyes lingered on the north from where the soldiers had come. "We will wait."

McGregor said, "You being a Texan, suh, do you know this part of the country?"

"Was up here once on a scout," Rhett said. "This is Kwahadi Comanche country, more or less."

"You think, suh, we might run onto some?"

"I'm hoping not."

"I heard tell they're more vicious than most other Injuns."

"They have that reputation, them and the Kiowas."

"Worse than the Cheyenne, I guess."

"By far," Rhett said. "Some of this country once belonged to the Apaches. You've heard about the Apaches?"

"I have heard some, yes, suh."

"The Comanches ran the Apaches out."

"Christ!"

"Gives you some idea."

The younger ones among the Kwahadies still protested. They pulled off by themselves, away from the older ones, and had a consultation.

Abruptly then, they wheeled about and raced their ponies southward after the bluebellies. The older ones stared after them, anger in their eyes.

The leader said, "Now we are only ten."

"We could join the young ones," another said.

The leader said, "No. They are fools, though brave with youth. They will be brave dead fools, soon enough."

"What then?"

"We will not join the young fools, but we will follow them. They would not mind my orders, but we will pick up their bodies."

"Their bodies!"

"Yes. And it is right that fools should die."

The six young braves began to fire as they came within weapons range of the pony soldiers. They were not as foolish as the older ones thought. The muscular youth who led them knew that the soldiers were loaded with visible supplies. And he had also noticed that the saddlebags draped behind their cantles sagged heavily. He knew that if pursued, he and his young braves, on their lightly burdened ponies, could quickly escape.

He had once lived for a time with the Penateka band of Comanches who had become agency Indians on the Clear Fork of the Brazos reservation. From that experience he had learned something of the white man's ways, so that he felt superior in knowledge to the elder braves.

He now wondered what might be hidden in those distended saddlebags. Coins? He knew how the white men valued those little flat circles of yellow metal.

He knew how easily weapons or whiskey could be bought with such baubles. If he and his young braves could bring down one of the whites and his horse, and drive off the others with pestering fire, he could learn if what he hoped about those saddlebags were true.

The battle was hidden from Rhett's men by a rolling contour, but the sound of rifle fire carried sufficiently to be heard.

"Hear that, Cap'n?" McGregor asked.

"I hear." Rhett kicked up the pace, then slowed as he began to top out the rise.

He was surprised by what he saw: a half dozen braves attacking over twenty bluebellies as the latter kept retreating, returning only sporadic fire.

And a half mile away from the scene, several other braves were sitting their mounts watching.

"What the hell is going on, Cap'n?"

"Don't know," Rhett said. "Beats any attack I ever saw."

"I thought them Cheyenne fought queer-like," McGregor said. "But this looks plumb crazy."

"Indian ways can be kind of strange, to our way of thinking," Rhett said.

At that moment one of the young braves shot a bluebelly's horse. The rider came free of his saddle, jerking free his carbine as he did so. He got off a shot at the braves before they riddled him with bullets.

His companions did not turn to help him. They kept on running.

"What kind of men are they?" McGregor said. "Them Yankees, I mean."

"Feeding the Comanches one sacrifice," Rhett said. "And hoping that'll satisfy."

"Will it?"

"I'm thinking not."

But the braves did ride to the fallen man and horse, and their muscular leader dismounted and reached for the saddlebags. He pulled out an ingot and held it, letting the sun glint on it. He appeared to say something then, and Rhett could guess at what he was saying.

"Telling them it's gold," Rhett said.

"You reckon they know the worth of gold?"

"I reckon that one does. And he's damn sure telling the others."

The young brave beckoned an invitation to the elder ones to join him, and after a hesitation they moved to do so. With help from his companions, the young leader detached the saddlebags from the dead horse and threw them over his own mount's withers. They all remounted then, and loped out fast again after the receding bluecoats. The older braves rode with them now.

"If the Yankees don't make a stand, the Injuns will pick them off one by one," McGregor said.

"If they make a stand," Rhett said, "the Comanches will just withdraw and wait till they move on. That young one in the lead is a smart one. Got white-man savvy, I'm thinking."

"Then they'll follow and keep picking men off," McGregor said. "Until they got the gold." He paused. "Cap'n, they get that gold, even weighted down with it, we'll never catch them on those Injun ponies."

"Doesn't leave us much choice, does it?"

"You mean, suh . . . "

"We'll have to help them."

"Help them goddamn Yankees, suh?"

"Like you said, if the Comanches get the gold, we'll never catch them," Rhett said. "Not in this country, where they know the land and we don't."

"I surely hate to do it, suh."

"We've got no choice," Rhett said. "Let's go!"

The Comanches were almost immediately aware of Rhett's men behind them but continued their own pursuit, not about to let the Yankees get away.

The rebels, at Rhett's orders, began firing their Spencers from the saddle. Their first shots hit nothing, then a single brave fell.

The other Comanches stopped, wheeled to face the rebels, and let the Yankees go.

"Damn Yankee fools!" Rhett said. And then he saw that Lieutenant Eilers realized what was going on. The Yankees halted, turned too, and charged the Comanche rear.

The two forces now had them in a crossfire, and dismounted to mow the Comanches down.

The young brave who had taken the saddlebags of ingots was knocked from his horse.

Rhett aimed at the horse and dropped it.

The surviving Comanches snatched up their dead and raced away to the west, leaving the saddlebags lying in the dust, partly weighted by the carcass of the pony.

The opposing forces ceased firing and stared at each other, weighing the possibilities.

McGregor said, "Well, suh, I reckon those saddlebags laying there are ours now."

The firing from both sides had been at maximum effective range, and now the range between the forces was double that. Rhett and Eilers both stood in the open, facing each other. Neither could read the other's expression. Each waited for some sign or movement.

"You want I should ride out and get those bags, suh?"

"You want to die?"

"You think they'd shoot, after what we just done for them?"

"I know it," Rhett said.

"Will they ride off and leave them?"

"I doubt it."

"We going to fight them for it?"

"They've still got us outnumbered three to two."

"Then why don't they take it?"

"They're not sure we'll stand for that, I reckon," Rhett said.

"Will they attack?"

"I doubt that. They'll not risk losing more men if they can help it. They need the men to bluff their way through to the border."

A Yankee began riding out from the group. Immediately, and with drill precision, the rest split and flanked him a few paces behind.

In the lead of one flank was Lieutenant Eilers.

"Do we open fire when they get within effective range?" Sergeant McGregor said.

"No," Rhett said. "Back off. We'll keep our distance unless they make a charge."

They retreated slowly as the Yankees progressed toward the dead Comanche pony and the saddlebags pinned partly beneath it. Rhett kept looking over his shoulder, as did most of the rebels.

The Yankee at formation point reached the horse, dismounted, and tugged at the bags but could not get them loose. Three of the others got down then and pulled at the carcass until the bags were freed.

The point man's mount appeared to be less burdened than the others, and he threw the saddlebags over its back. He got up in his saddle and they all pivoted and rode away, heading south once more.

All except Lieutenant Eilers, who sat his horse watching Rhett. Then, as his men left him, he suddenly raised his hand in what could have been a salute of thanks or a gesture of defiance.

"You think he's thanking us?" McGregor said.

"Who knows? He damned sure ought to be." Rhett paused. "It's more like he knows what our own plans are. Knows we want him to get the gold to the border for us. And like us, he's agreeable there. Knows if he can keep what men he's got, he has a better chance of success."

"How are we going to get it from him then?"

Rhett shrugged. "We'll have to meet that problem when we come to it. Right now we've got to make sure we don't lose track of him. Once we reach the border, the showdown will have to come."

CHAPTER 15

RHETT did not like the role he was playing, the role he had determined was the most expedient way for him to get the bullion through violent postwar Texas. He did not like it and he knew his men did not like it, but there was reluctant agreement among them that the role was necessary. He and his rebels had to ride escort, more or less, for the hated band of bluebelly deserters.

He was further irritated by his strong suspicion that Lieutenant Eilers was amused. Ever since the renegade Coloradan officer had raised his arm in what was surely a mocking gesture after the aborted Comanche attack, Rhett had fretted about this.

Eilers would be enjoying this unique protection from attack. Until the final one, of course, when the border was reached and crossed. Even then, it was Rhett who had the worry. How would he overpower Eilers's larger force?

When the time came, he, Rhett, would have to pounce fast, before the band of deserters split up with the loot and disappeared into the desolate wilds of Mexico.

They had ridden a few miles behind their quarry for several days, and on reduced rations their tempers were getting worse. There was much grumbling now, as the never-satisfied hunger of the men wore away at ragged nerves.

Even McGregor grew sullen. "Suh," the sergeant said, "I've no liking to be riding empty-bellied, knowing them murdering bastards up ahead are eating up the lion's share of those provisions they took from Fort Murrah."

150

Rhett said nothing. He had no reasonable comment to make on that.

They crossed the San Saba and were in broken country, scattered prairies and clear streams. Fair cattle country, Rhett thought, and remembered his own ranch days only a little to the east, but so far away in time when viewed through the intervening years of war.

He wondered if Eilers would risk an approach toward San Antonio, and half wished that he would. In that direction, whatever the risk, there was a chance of getting supplies.

But Eilers, having taken heavily of the foodstuffs stored at Murrah, did not have Rhett's urgent need, and kept a heading that would take them a hundred miles or more west of the old town.

A couple of days later Rhett, riding in the lead as usual, topped out a ridge and stared down through the summer heat waves at an afternoon encampment of the deserters. It was a sprawled and careless blotch on a bank above a sluggish flow of the upper Nueces River. The undulating country here was filled with brakes of cedar.

Some of the hardcases were splashing naked in the water.

Eilers seemed almost to be flaunting a measured lack of concern. If there were pickets posted, they had to be hidden in the cedars, Rhett thought. The son of a bitch has it all figured out, Rhett thought, his ire rising.

McGregor seemed to match Rhett's reaction. He said, "Suh, can't we attack them? Leastwise try to pick off a few to bring down the odds? It can't be too much farther to the border."

"I'm considering it," Rhett said. Still, he thought, Eilers wasn't a fool. He began to count those of Eilers's men he could see. He counted only ten. The others must be hidden in the brakes. At least, they were out of sight.

It was then that Trooper Brogden came up beside them

and spoke with quiet urgency: "Riders coming behind us, suh. Seven of them."

Rhett turned and saw them riding openly up the slope. "Stay alert," he said. "Mac, pass the word to the others."

McGregor nodded and moved away, leading his horse.

Rhett handed his reins to Brogden and stood facing the approaching men. They were wearing nondescript clothing, but they sat their saddles with cavalry ease.

As they drew close, the rebels raised their carbines to the ready, but the horsemen did not slow.

And now Rhett was struck by a vague familiarity about the one who suddenly spurred a few paces into the lead.

This one halted ten yards away, keeping his hands on his saddle pommel, as did his companions. "Well, Cap'n," he said, his strong voice carrying.

Rhett fought the impulse to glance over his shoulder, fearful those down in the encampment could have heard. He kept his eyes on the man before him and said, "Speak quiet."

"There's a reason?"

"There could be."

"Well, then, suppose I ride closer."

"Come ahead, but keep your hands in sight."

"That I'll do, you can be sure, sir. What with a dozen carbines aiming on me." He had a Missouri accent. He rode five yards nearer. "You're looking well, Cap'n Rhett."

Rhett was startled. He kept studying the man, annoyed that he couldn't place the faint familiarity of the face.

"Been nigh a year, Cap'n. Last saw you in Mizzoura. Boonville, to be exact. You was with Pap Price, and I and these men was with Bloody Bill Anderson. We had us one hell of a celebration, if'n you remember?"

Rhett remembered that Boonville's small Federal garrison had fallen easily. And Bloody Bill and three hundred of his guerrillas had ridden in from massacring the town of Centralia a week before in an orgy of atrocities.

Confederate regulars like Rhett had been sickened by the boasting of Bloody Bill's guerrillas. Thinking of the way these bushwhacking bastards had gloated over those atrocities sickened him even now. They had ambushed a hundred and fifty northern militiamen, killing all including those who surrendered.

Then, spurred on by a vicious madness, they beheaded the corpses and switched them to different bodies. Some heads they stuck on fence posts. They scalped others of the dead and dying, or cut off noses and ears for souvenirs.

They even bragged of slicing off the genitals of a still-living officer and stuffing them into his mouth.

"You remember, Cap'n?"

"I might have seen you in Boonville," Rhett said. "You look some familiar to me."

"I remember you well," the guerrilla said. "You was wearing a sergeant's coat, but somebody told me you was a captain. I remembered because I got a kick out of that, thinking if'n I wasn't told I sure wouldn't've knowed. Meaning that, stripped to the skin, one man ain't no better than another, I reckon."

Rhett said curtly, "State your business."

"Name of Job, Cap'n. Rob Job."

"Odd name."

"Ain't it, though?" The guerrilla leader grinned. "Kind of fits what I do best now. Jobs of robbing and such-like."

"So?"

Job shrugged. "Me and the boys here pushed on west, now the war is over. We heard it was the land of opportunity, especial for our kind who are handy with guns."

Rhett waited.

"Went too far west, maybe," Job said. "Leastwise we ain't found the opportunity we been looking for. Not till now, maybe. We run onto a old man in a little stockade a few days back and we been following your tracks ever since."

"Why?"

"Why? Because that old man—after we got through asking him polite-like—was right interesting to talk to. Gave us your name, number of men you had, said you was ex-rebels, and so on. Also that you was trailing a couple of dozen Yankee deserters for reasons of your own."

"What did you do to that old man?" Rhett said, his voice hard with anger.

"Didn't take much. Cuffed him around a little. That's when he let slip he'd peeked into one them saddlebags the Yankees was toting. Seen a gold bar. Seems that over half them Yanks was loaded likewise. Right away, I took on a thought. The thought led me to thinking."

"Thinking what?"

"Thinking if them Yank deserters are carrying gold, and you been trailing them, the reason is clear." Job paused. "Thought came, too, that they got you outnumbered. Thinking on that thought, I figured you could use some help."

Rhett thought about it. Finally, he said, "Light down."

"Sure, Cap'n. Say, how you fixed for grub?"

"Short-rationed," Rhett said. He looked at the sacks on the bushwhackers' mounts.

Job grinned. He had a young-old face that was mean even with the grin. "Be our guests. We took all that old man had left. The invite, though, only applies if'n you choose our offer of help."

"We've already eaten," Rhett said.

Job swung down from his saddle, and his men followed suit. "Now, Cap'n, you think it over first. You think it over real good. A man like you, a officer and all in the Confederate States of America Regular Army, he ought to be able to see the good that could come from having us join you."

Rhett was silent, thinking of the Yankee deserters just over the ridge. He did not speak of them. Not right away.

The rebels, who had been listening to the talk between the two leaders, stared with suspicion and loathing at the new arrivals. The guerrillas stared back, and some of them grinned without amusement. They were accustomed to this kind of reception. They had, over the years of Kansas-Missouri border warfare, come to pride themselves on the revulsion they evoked in southern regulars.

They remembered that the Confederate Army commanders had nevertheless been quick enough to utilize their services when a campaign got underway. Hadn't Pap Price himself conferred an honorary colonel's rank on Quantrill, Bloody Bill's mentor?

Rhett noted the guerrillas' weapons, unorthodox from a regular's view, but devastatingly effective in bushwhack warfare. Each of Job's men had a carbine in a saddle scabbard, but to them this was a secondary weapon. Quantrill's men, as well as Bloody Bill Anderson's, had relied for firepower on revolvers, most favored being the five- or six-shot navy Colts. Each of Job's men wore two on his belt, and two more were in special saddle holsters.

In the short, vicious cavalry charges of the foliaged Missouri countryside, which was their primary habitat throughout the war, the guerrillas had learned that enemy troopers armed with cumbersome longer weapons were no match for them.

All this Rhett was considering as his own men shot him occasional sidelong glances, waiting for his decision.

Rhett met Job's eyes across the space that separated the two groups of men. He saw the supercilious grin that tugged at Job's hard mouth, and he hated himself for what he had decided to do.

"All right," he said, and saw Job's grin widen, and felt his rancor grow.

"You'll not regret it, Cap'n." The grin reached the guerrilla chief's eyes. "You know that, don't you?"

Rhett did not answer.

"You understand, though, we'll want a fair share of that gold after we help you take it."

"I considered that," Rhett said.

"Just so it's understood."

Rhett nodded. The time might be right, he had decided. The time to try for the gold. He had been wondering how he could ever overpower Eilers's force, and now he felt, with reluctance, that he must accept this offer of help.

There would be trouble afterward, he was sure. But he'd deal with that when it occurred.

"Just how far ahead are them Yankee bastards, Cap'n?" Job said.

Rhett gestured for the guerrilla to follow. He moved up toward the skyline, then lay prone and waited for Job's comment.

"By God!" the bushwhacker said. "Ain't that enticing!"

"It won't be easy."

"Nothing's easy," Job said. "They seasoned troopers?"

"Sand Creek killers."

The guerrilla momentarily turned his head, showing surprise. "I heard about them." He grinned again. "My kind of men."

"Yeah," Rhett said. "Exactly."

"Be glad we are what we are, Cap'n. It takes fire to fight fire." The guerrilla turned back to studying the scene below. After a pause, he said, "What's your plan?"

"What would be yours?"

"Me and the boys love fast action, and we love killing, Cap'n. We always fight one way, if the odds are anywise near even. We go in charging, with guns firing, and kill or be killed."

Rhett knew this was so. He had witnessed guerrillas in action in Missouri, and like most regulars he considered them maniacs, men with souls warped by blood-soak of their enemies and even themselves.

"No quarter given and none asked," Job said. "We never fight no other way."

Rhett said, "We'll work our way into position. We go charging down from here, they'll be waiting for us."

"You're in command, Cap'n. Only when we get close, there'll be no holding back my men. It'll be devil take the hindmost."

Rhett nodded. "Listen, don't be shooting us by mistake. They're wearing cavalry yellow piping, we've got infantry white."

"Yes, *sir!*"

Rhett gave the guerrilla a quick look, but the man's face was unreadable. He didn't trust Job at all. He hesitated, then said, "Let's go!"

When they were all mounted, Job bunched his men slightly to the rear.

McGregor pushed his way to Rhett, followed by Private Brogden.

"We will try to take the gold," Rhett said.

"Against over twenty troopers, suh?" Brogden said.

"The odds are even now."

Brogden gave the guerrillas a suspicious glance, but he made no further comment.

McGregor did. He said in a low voice, "Do they know our destination, suh?"

"No," Rhett said.

Job must have overheard, because his hard grin returned, and he called to McGregor, "We're all rebels, friend."

"This is Sergeant McGregor," Rhett said. "My second in command."

Job nodded and said, "Sergeant." He rode close to join them.

"We'll get close as we can, try for surprise," Rhett said.

"Then we charge," Job said, still grinning. "Right, sir?"

"Yeah, but don't anybody fire first. Leave that to me."

"You're giving the orders, sir."

Rhett led them westward a quarter mile, making certain they stayed below the skyline. He then halted, dismounted, and worked his way to the crest. Upstream from where the renegade bluecoats were bivouacked, there were several large brakes of cedar to give cover. A bit farther west from Rhett's position, a slanting draw led down from the high ground almost to the riverbed before disappearing into one of these brakes.

He went back to the waiting men and remounted. They continued on until they reached the top of the draw. Rhett turned down, riding slowly, fearful that the sound of clanking metal would give warning to the enemy. He had already stressed the need for voice silence.

They reached the bottom and paused in the brake, listening. They could still hear the men cavorting in the river, and by this they were reassured.

They worked their way downstream then, always keeping a screening of cedar or other foliage for cover.

The sound of the cavorting troopers was close now, and Rhett halted again. Job pulled up beside him and said in a low voice, "We'll surprise hell out of them."

"I'm not so sure," Rhett said. "Those bathers been splashing a long time. Too long, maybe."

He had just spoken when from directly across the river shallows and out of a brake, carbines blasted and a guerrilla was knocked from his saddle. The horse of a rebel Yankee reared as a bullet seared its rump, and a guerrilla mount went to its knees, then toppled as its rider leaped free. The rider moved fast and caught the reins of the riderless horse of his fallen comrade, swung up on the saddle.

"They knew we were coming," McGregor said. "They set us a trap."

Job heard this. His grin was gone. He signaled his five remaining men, and they formed a wide-spaced line, drove spurs into their mounts and charged across the river, the shallow water splashing high. Each held his reins in his teeth, firing from a revolver in either hand.

Rhett rode at their heels, followed by his rebels.

Those magnificent, bloodthirsty, maniacal guerrilla bastards! he thought. Those dirty, rotten, cruel, degenerate, murdering, brave sons of bitches! They had no regard for life, enemy or their own.

And the Sand Creek killers in the thicket, shocked by the insane attack they had ignited, panicked, fired wild misses, and were overwhelmed.

These were no unarmed Cheyenne squaws and kids they were facing now. Within seconds, four out of six hidden in the thicket were dead. The other two broke and ran and were overtaken by the guerrillas who rode recklessly into the brake and blasted their heads apart from the distance of a yard.

Rhett knew now that he had something to fear from these insane killers who no longer functioned as even remotely reasonable men. They craved blood as some men craved whiskey.

They were in love with death.

Job turned his head and met Rhett's glance. He grinned again, a vicious, ecstatic grin like none Rhett had ever seen on the face of a man in combat.

Still grinning, Job called, "Let's hit them that's down the river, Cap'n," and without waiting for Rhett to answer, he wheeled about and led his men in that direction.

Rhett felt obliged to follow.

There was no sound now from Eilers's position. No more playful noise from frolicking men. The fusillade of moments before had brought instant silence.

Eilers would be waiting, Rhett thought, and then was sure of it as they broke out into the clearing and the Sand Creekers opened up.

Once again the ill-trained deserters broke and ran, no match for the battle-hardened guerrillas.

But Eilers was no fool. He was an experienced Indian-fighter, and had faced other unpredictable behavior by his enemies in battle. His remaining men opened up from flanking thickets on either side and caught Job's guerrillas in a crossfire.

Poor marksmanship by the Sand Creekers saved the bush-whackers—that and Rhett's directing answering fire into the flank attackers as the guerrillas drove on to ride down the fleeing enemy in front of them.

In a matter of minutes the Sand Creekers were down, dead or wounded, or they were raising their hands, foolishly, in surrender, to be cut down by the Missourians.

All except Eilers, who was crouched in a strew of boulders, making a last, hopeless stand, a soldier to the end.

A bullet from Rhett's revolver caught him in the chest, knocking him back and down.

Rhett reined up sharply and saw that Eilers had lost his weapon. He was of a mind to give the Coloradan a coup de grace in retaliation for what he or his men had done to Corporal Hall.

But then the renegade lieutenant's eyes rose to stare at Rhett and his lips formed words. Eilers moved his head from side to side, and his voice reached Rhett, startlingly strong for a dying man.

"You goddamned fool," Eilers gasped. "Teaming up with those kind. . . . You got the gold . . . but how long can you keep it?"

His head fell back then, and Rhett let his hand drop. There was no need for the gun now.

But Eilers's words stuck with him.

CHAPTER 16

JOB'S guerrillas went among the wounded, finishing them off with bullets to the head.

Rhett protested.

"What would you have us do, Cap'n?" Job said tightly. "Leave them to slow-die where they lay? Hell, we're just putting them out of their misery. You'd do that much for a horse." He stopped long enough to give Rhett a grin. "If you don't have the stomach for it, look the other way."

Rhett's face hardened, but he had no reply. There was nowhere they could take the wounded. Not expediently. And expedience now was becoming more and more the determining factor in Rhett's own thinking. *Get the gold to Shelby.* He had to keep that foremost in his mind.

But some of his men dismounted and walked out of sight to retch.

He ignored this. He had to give credit to the guerrillas that the Sand Creekers were annihilated, and that he had not lost a man of his own. His total casualties were three troopers with minor wounds.

The guerrillas were brutal and fearless. Rhett became painfully aware that in a showdown with them, he would lose men. With three wounded, he had ten able-bodied against Job's six, but even with these odds he did not want a face-off with them. It would be better to share some of the gold than to see his men die.

Job was not slow in bringing up the subject. "Well, Cap'n, I reckon it's time to share the spoils. We just been peeking into them saddlebags these Yankees was carrying. Ain't no wonder you been on their trail."

Job's men had gathered about him, and each, including Job, had transferred a pair of bags from the Yankees' mounts to his own. And each was leading a Yankee mount carrying another pair.

"Hold on!" Rhett said. "We've been a long time tracking that metal."

"And we're the ones that took it for you," Job said. "It rightly belongs all to us now. But being a fair-minded man, and you being southern boys like us, we're willing to accept only what we figure is fair."

"You've got twenty-four out of twenty-six bags!" Rhett exclaimed.

"So we have, Cap'n, so we have. Just so happened it worked out that way. Of course we could lead one more extra animal and take it all. But I figure fair is fair, and we're leaving you a couple for your ownself, you being the commanding officer, so to speak."

"You're insane!"

"That we are, Cap'n, that we are. And it'll be well for you to remember it." Job leered. "Now them bars is each got a seventy-five stamped on it, meaning pounds, I reckon. So them two we're leaving you is near forty thousand dollars' worth, more or less. Split with your men, that's about three thousand a piece. A damned good grubstake, I'd say. You don't want to be greedy, Cap'n."

"Jesus!" McGregor said.

"You may not agree," Job continued. "In that case we'll fight you for it, here and now. You make the decision, Cap'n."

Rhett said nothing.

Job said quickly, "Else we'll just ride out with our gold, remaining friends after a profitable relationship. What say?"

"Looks like you're taking all the profit."

"Why, Cap'n, you're near forty thousand dollars richer."

"Reckon I don't have much choice," Rhett said.

Job nodded. "Reckon you don't."

"So be it," Rhett said.

His men watched bitterly as the six mounted guerrillas, each leading a loaded spare mount, prepared to leave.

"Just one thing more," Job said. "I trust you as a honorable regular officer. But just to make sure, throw down all your weapons on the ground there. Again you have a choice. You can draw and fire, and at least six of you will die." He paused. "I'm waiting, Cap'n."

Rhett said, "You may ride out, but you'll do it while we're armed."

Job's grin held. "Don't much blame you for that. I wouldn't trust us none neither, was I you."

"My thought exactly."

"Tell you what you do, Cap'n, less'n you choose to fight and lose a lot of men. You ride out into that open stretch off there to the east, and stay there out of range. We'll keep our eye on you. And don't go getting rash."

Rhett made no comment.

"Just remember," Job said, "what we done to all these bluebellies."

"Not likely I'll forget it."

"Start riding."

Rhett gestured to his men and they headed for the extensive open space. When he looked back, he could see the guerrillas riding southward down the Nueces. They'd strike the trail down there somewhere that led westerly to Eagle Pass and Piedras Negras, he was thinking. That's if they didn't choose to split up.

If they split, he'd lose them. But if they hung together, it would give him a chance to strike back. He was determined to retrieve the gold. It had been a gambler's decision not to shoot it out when Job offered his dare. Rhett was gambling on luck to keep the bushwhackers together until they reached the border. But what was it that Jed Evans, the storekeeper at Cheyenne Springs, had said? That "luck can get you killed"?

Thought of Evans brought back memory of Sherry. The memory stabbed him like a knife. Had he been a fool to put his mission ahead of his love for her? He was beginning to think so. At that moment he felt an overpowering urge to turn back. And knew that he could never go back. Too much had happened, including his desertion, and now the slaughter of Lieutenant Eilers and his men. Sand Creekers or not, they had been Union troops. His part in their death would not be excused, not after he had pledged to wear the blue himself.

He allowed himself one final thought, before he brought himself back to the present. He wondered if Sherry would marry Evans, for he knew that Evans longed to make her his wife.

McGregor interrupted his thought. "We going to follow them, suh?"

"Yes, Mac."

"Begging your pardon, suh, but I don't understand why you let them get away with this."

"What would you have done?"

"I don't know, suh, for sure. But I think I'd have gone for our guns and had it out when he challenged us. We had them outnumbered."

"I believed what he said. We'd have lost at least a half dozen men, the way they handle those revolvers. Even if we killed them all off in return, I did not consider that a good trade-off."

"So what do we do now, suh?"

"We'll pick them off one at a time along the trail. With carbines. Our kind of weapon, not theirs. Close up, like they were, we were no match for their specialty, which is handguns."

McGregor's spirits seemed to lift, then settled once more.

He stared at the single set of gold-bar bags slung behind Rhett's saddle. "Hell!" he said.

"At long range we'll have the advantage," Rhett said. "We've got our Spencer repeaters. Did you notice the carbines they were carrying?"

"I didn't, suh. I didn't see them using theirs."

"Perry Brass Frame, single-shot, breech-loaders. No match in a firefight with ours."

The sergeant's face still looked perturbed. "One other thing, suh. If they go separate ways, how do we follow?"

"I don't think that will happen before they cross the border. If they head for Eagle Pass, we've got a hundred or better miles in which to wipe them out. And leading extra horses with gold loads, they won't be moving fast."

"Yes, suh," McGregor said. "I see how you come by your decision."

"Keep your fingers crossed, Sergeant."

CHAPTER 17

ON July 4, General Jo Shelby had led several hundred men, the remnants of his Iron Brigade, to the banks of the Rio Grande at Eagle Pass.

He halted there and sat his horse, staring across the river at the Mexican town of Piedras Negras.

A corporal carrying the tattered Stars and Bars, his battle flag that had never dipped in surrender, rode up beside him.

Then, with a roll of drums and the notes from a bugle, the flag, weighted by a boulder, was lowered into the muddy waters of the river.

The men, standing at attention, were then aware that Shelby had changed his intentions. He would not lead them to a base from which to continue to attack the Union. Something had happened during the months he had lingered in Texas. Perhaps he had seen at last the futility of it all.

Now he was simply leading them into exile, in a still-adamant refusal to submit to the arrogant northern conquerors.

None of them knew what lay ahead. But those here assembled were ready to follow him, no matter what he was planning.

Mexico was now immersed in a civil war of its own. The forces of Emperor Maximilian, an Austrian archduke placed on a phantom throne by Napoléon III, and backed by invading French legions, was pitted everywhere against the ousted President Benito Juárez.

There was a rumor that the general would offer the

services of the brigade in exchange for Maximilian's help in exacting honorable conditions and amnesties for the hotspur Confederates. Which could be a far better settlement than what had been offered those southerners who had surrendered.

They rode down the sandy riverbank and crossed to Piedras Negras. Their first destination would be Monterrey, a couple hundred miles of rock-cropped brushland away, miles of desolate daytime heat and nighttime cold.

And at Monterrey they were stopped by Maximilian's French commander in the area, General Pierre Jeanningros. Jeanningros, with hundreds of French Legionnaires and Mexican auxiliary troops, surrounded Shelby's smaller force.

Jeanningros sent word that Shelby could proceed no farther.

Shelby's hotspur temper rose and he issued an ultimatum of his own. If he were not allowed to proceed on his way to see Maximilian in Mexico City, he would attack with the light weapons he had. "Shall it be peace or war between us?" Shelby demanded.

His defiant courage impressed the French commander, a seasoned campaigner himself. He invited Shelby to a conference.

When he asked how Shelby could dare to threaten an attack against an encirclement of heavy weaponry, Shelby drew himself up stiffly and said, "You seem to forget, sir, that we still have our side arms."

The French general ended up throwing a banquet for Shelby and his officers, and sent him on his way.

In August, Maximilian granted Shelby an audience in the magnificent Chapultepec Palace in Mexico City. The young emperor, of Austrian blood, a tall man, and not uncongenial, treated him with courtesy.

Shelby offered his command in the service of the emperor.

The emperor refused.

Shelby pointed out his belief that the United States would now move to enforce the Monroe Doctrine against foreign infringement in Latin America, and would soon seek to oust the French. France would have to get out of Mexico or fight the U.S., against whom Shelby and his Confederates had been warring for four years.

They could join forces.

But Maximilian told him he would not tolerate an armed force in Mexico aside from his own troops, French or Mexican. He was not interested in fighting the United States. He was, instead, anxious to gain its goodwill.

And so Shelby realized at last that his dream of carrying on the fight against the Yankees was ended.

"You may stay as individuals, but not as soldiers," the emperor said. "You were an agrarian people in your own South, with great experience in cotton, coffee, sugarcane, and field crops. Now, if you wish, I will set aside land on which you can live in your own agricultural colonies."

Shelby knew then that he had to disband his troops.

In September, two months after Shelby had crossed the Rio Grande, Maximilian issued a land decree that authorized the Confederates to move to the region inland from Veracruz, on the lush tropical eastern slopes of the Mexican *cordillera*, close to the Caribbean Sea, and start their colonies.

Maximilian granted General Shelby the use of a fine hacienda expropriated from the now-exiled General López de Santa Anna. The hotspur general soon returned to the life of a southern planter.

The men of the Iron Brigade were not all satisfied with this. They had crossed the border with the intent to fight, not engage in agriculture.

Now, seeing their intentions thwarted, many hoped the U.S. Government would make it safe for them to return to what was left of their homes. But the radical reconstruction politicians and the carpetbaggers saw it to their advantage to exact the ultimate forfeiture from the rebels. They would make them beg for pardons for having done what they thought was their constitutional right—to secede from the Union.

And that was more than southern pride could bear.

The adventurous among them disappeared into the wild reaches of Mexico. They were glimpsed sometimes in Guaymas, on the Sea of Cortez, before slipping into Arizona or California; in Mazatlán, on the Pacific, from where they shipped for God-knows-where.

They were seen prospecting northwest of San Luis Potosí in the province of that name. They met sometimes in Campeche, and even in the jungles of Yucatán. Few of these ever returned to the states for which they had fought so bitterly.

There were others, desperate and bold and reckless, who defied the Mexican *juaristas* now holding a zone fifty miles deep along the boundary, and slipped through or fought through to cross into Texas . . . to live there without amnesty, whatever the hazards, in the hated reconstruction environment.

Many of these burned with resentment, not only for the merciless northern government, but for Shelby himself and his fellow commanders who had raised their hopes, then let them down.

And Shelby, it seemed to many, was caught up in a vision of a transplanted homeland, southern-style, his great plan to fight on abandoned; although there still smoldered a hate for having lost his plantations in Missouri and Kentucky.

He summed up his feeling in a letter to a friend:

I am here as an exile; defeated by the acts of the Southern people themselves. And why? Because they loved their estates more than principle. . . . Let them reap what they deserved, eternal disgrace. Damn them, they were foolish enough to think by laying down their arms they would enjoy all the rights they once had. . . . My heart is heavy at the thought of being separated from you all forever; but I am not one of those to ask forgiveness for that which I believe even today is right. The party in power has manifested no leniency.

CHAPTER 18

THEY killed their first guerrilla within ten miles.

Rhett personally shot the guerrilla out of his saddle. It did not bother him to do so, and it was only later that he became aware of this. The guerrillas had been unwanted allies, but they had enabled him to vanquish Eilers and his Sand Creekers. Still, he felt he owed them nothing, not after they had taken away the gold.

All the hell he had gone through to get this far—it had hardened him to this cold-blooded killing.

It had been simple enough, so simple that he wondered now at Job's stupidity not to think this would happen. Where in hell was the guerrilla leader's strategy?

He and the rebels had simply ridden up to within effective range, and he had picked off the trailing rider with his carbine.

He was not surprised that the cold killing did not concern him. He was going to complete his mission, no matter what it took. He had sacrificed already his honor and the woman he loved, and by God, the mere killing of southern guerrillas would not stand in his way!

They shot the second guerrilla a few miles after the first.

This time it was Sergeant McGregor who pulled the trigger.

The man tumbled out of his saddle just as had the first, and again the loaded animals were caught up by a guerrilla who grabbed the fallen rider's reins and dashed into cover leading three horses.

But McGregor did not stomach it as well as Rhett had

done. He looked sick and pale, and finally said, "My God, suh! I don't like this. Picking them off in cold blood—I don't have the stomach for it. After all, they were on our side a short time back."

"That gold goes to the Confederacy," Rhett said. His voice had a strained quality that the sergeant had never heard before.

"Fighting is one thing," McGregor said. "This is murder, suh."

"So has been the whole goddamned war," Rhett said.

"This is different, suh." The sergeant startled himself by his insubordination, but he seemed more shocked by the bitter change he saw in Rhett's behavior. Had the captain's single-minded obsession to accomplish his aborted mission caused this change? McGregor now believed it had.

The captain had given up the woman he loved for this, and McGregor suspected that this weighed heavily on the captain's mind. It could crack a man, he guessed. Such a sacrifice could make all other feelings seem unimportant. It could leave a man with nothing left but a cold dedication to his goal.

"What we're doing, suh," McGregor said, "makes us no better than those guerrillas we are killing."

Rhett scowled. "You didn't object when I told you the plan, after they robbed us."

The sergeant nodded his head. "No, suh, I didn't. Then it was talk. But now that it's being done, I feel different. Particular since they are rightly southern boys."

"Get a grip on yourself, Sergeant. It's got to be."

"It's a cost to pay," said the sergeant.

"And goddammit, I'm paying the cost!" Rhett said, voice rising.

"Yes, suh. And I been seeing it happen."

"Seeing what?"

"Seeing you change into a man with a obsession, suh. Seeing you give up your word of honor to the Yankee government." The sergeant paused. "Well, we all did that. On account of the gold." He hesitated, then said, "And seeing you trade that doctor lady that loved you for this, suh."

"I don't want to hear about it," Rhett said.

"Sure you don't. And now you got to be no better than those bushwhacking guerrillas you're murdering. You even got me doing it, and I'm sick I listened to your order to do so. I tell you, Cap'n, I will not kill another one that way."

"It's war, Sergeant. *And that gold has got to be taken to General Shelby.*"

"Does it, now, suh?" McGregor shook his head. "Only because you say so. You've had this in your mind so long, you've lost your reason, suh."

"I hand-picked you men to help me on this mission," Rhett said.

McGregor did not answer at once. Then he said, "Cap'n, have you forgot that half the men was of a mind to join with Corporal Hall, back there when them Cheyenne Dog Soldiers was riding to attack that town?"

"You saw what happened to Hall," Rhett said.

"Might not have, if there'd been more of us sided him instead of obeying your wishes. At that time maybe we still had some thought of duty, of protecting that doctor lady and them other townsfolk. Maybe you still had a stronger hold on us. And maybe we figured we'd get a later chance at the gold."

"We've got it now," Rhett said.

"Things have changed, Cap'n. From the beginning, there wasn't a man of us hasn't been thinking of how it'd be to get a share of that gold for his ownself."

"*That gold belongs to the Confederacy,*" Rhett said.

"For what? To carry on a lost war? Suh, you are one of a kind, and I've looked up to you for that reason. But I tell you now, you are a damned fool if you think these men are going to give up their dream to be rich."

"Not even for the honor of the South?"

"Not even for that, suh. And if you weren't a man obsessed, you'd realize it."

Rhett's face became ugly. "I always believed I could trust you men to think of the Confederacy first."

"Not where a fortune in gold is concerned, Cap'n."

"And you, Sergeant? Are you like the others?"

"I'm afraid so, suh."

"I had my doubts about Corporal Hall," Rhett said, "but I thought you were different."

"I'm afraid not, suh. Not when it comes to gold."

"Would you kill those other 'southern boys' if you were going to keep a split of the gold, Sergeant?"

McGregor was again a long time in answering. He said finally, "It might be I would, suh."

"Makes a difference then, doesn't it? Greed or honor?"

"After four years of war, it surely does, suh. What makes a bigger difference—and you don't seem to understand—is that the *war is over!*"

"I still have faith in Shelby."

"You want to believe the war will continue, suh. That's what you've wanted so long you can't get it out of your head. But the rest of us, we only want to be shed of it."

"You'd kill for the gold. I'd kill for the Confederacy," Rhett said.

"The war is over," McGregor repeated. "We've got to look to our own futures now."

"I'm still in command here, Sergeant."

"Yes, suh," McGregor said. "But I can't guarantee how much longer your orders will be followed."

Rhett killed another one.

McGregor looked at him as if he'd crawled out from under a rock, but he said nothing. The rest of the men were silent too.

Rhett turned and caught their stares, and at that moment

a wave of self-revulsion struck him. It hit him suddenly and with great force, and he knew then what McGregor had been talking about.

He knew then that he could not continue, he could not do it again. Killing in the heat of battle was one thing; killing in cold blood, without danger to himself, was something else.

He abruptly felt as he had that other time when old Jim Bodine had fallen dead from the belfry at his feet.

McGregor eyed him critically and seemed to sense this. He said, "Had enough, suh?" McGregor's face was unforgiving.

Rhett made no answer. At the moment, he was beyond that.

But he was at a loss for what he would do now.

Job had realized too late his mistake in leaving the Galvanized Yankees to follow. He was raging that he had not forced a showdown with them. Still, thinking about it logically, he'd not had much choice. Not if he wanted to survive with enough men to carry away the gold.

But now, with three killed out of the six of them, he had to do something. If that goddamned cavalry officer sniped one more man . . .

The problem, of course, was that he was vastly outnumbered now. This was something to which he was not accustomed. Through the years of fighting in Missouri and Kansas, his guerrillas had run in sizable bunches, always seeking the odds against their victims. Now, being on the short end, his prior experience offered him no real solution.

Still, he recalled a time or two when he and his kind had fought their way out of a tight situation by sheer viciousness.

It had worked against ill-trained northern militia, and even Kansas Jayhawker units now and then. Here, he was up against seasoned regulars, and that could make it tougher.

But he had to take the chance. The alternative was extinction. And, by God, he wasn't going to let that bastard captain snuff him out! Not when he had a half million dollars in gold in his possession, with which to buy a life of luxurious ease.

He was fed up with the meager pickings to be taken now in the impoverished, beaten South. He was going to live rich or die trying.

The Texan captain was a leader, though. He must be, to have kept a dozen men dedicated to a lost cause. Job knew there wasn't a man among them that didn't have a personal, driving interest in that gold.

The target, then, was the captain. He'd concentrate on killing Rhett. There could then be a fight among the rest of the regulars that would give him a chance to still get away with the wealth.

Well, he knew only one way to fight. Bloody Bill Anderson's way. Quantrill had got more fame, but Bloody Bill made Quantrill look like a Sunday-school teacher, when you compared them on the basis of pure viciousness.

Job had been a right fair pupil of Anderson's. Not top leader material, maybe. Wasn't smart enough, Bill had told him to his face one time. But, by God, he was mean enough! And that's what really counted. Job found himself grinning, although he wasn't yet quite sure why.

The guerrillas had disappeared.

McGregor said, "Where you reckon they went, suh?"

The country here had become hilly.

"They could double back in this terrain," Rhett said. "I want flankers on alert and men guarding our rear."

"You think they'd attack us with so few men, Cap'n?"

"They did it on the Coloradans."

"They didn't do it alone, though, suh."

"Desperate men, Sergeant. It's the way they've fought for years."

"God help the poor sons of bitches!"

"God help us if they take us by surprise. Get those flankers out."

Job had discovered a tiny valley and picketed all the loaded pack animals. He then rode back through the cluster of hills with his two surviving men. The smirk on his face was fixed.

His men, seeing this, grew ever more excited. When Job grinned, they had come to expect anything. He didn't grin like other men did.

They knew he was crazy. He had been that way for years. Ever since some Kansas Jayhawkers had set fire to his farmhouse in Missouri while he was away, burning his wife and children alive.

They followed him now because that was their habit. Each knew death rode at his elbow, but none was perturbed. They had each ridden with that companion so long that familiarity had bred contempt.

They did not attack on Rhett's flanks or rear at all.

At the moment Rhett sighted the magnificent bastards, they were rounding a bend in a shallow ravine directly ahead, and two hundred yards away. Their disregard for life stunned him almost into withholding fire.

Then he remembered how they'd annihilated the Sand Creekers, and, in near panic, he drew his revolver and shot. It did no harm at that distance, but it signaled a carbine volley from his men, and it was over. The last three guerrillas lay dead.

And the gold was once more his.

But he felt no exultation.

CHAPTER 19

NOW they had the gold and the Rio Grande was before them.

And Sergeant McGregor, his tones suddenly hard, said, "I reckon, suh, that here is where we part company."

"I don't think so," Rhett said.

"You can't fight us all, Cap'n." The sergeant's voice contained an element of regret. "Much as we've come to respect you, suh, the men have all agreed on this." He paused. "We will each take the share we're carrying and go our own way." He paused again. "It will work out for the best that way, suh—us spreading out. Just in case there's anybody trying to trace us. You can see that, can't you, suh?"

"But the gold belongs to the Confederacy, not us," Rhett said. "You men are missing the whole point of our objective."

"*Your* objective, suh, not ours. Much as I admire your loyalty to the cause, suh, me and the others ain't made of the stuff you are. Meaning we each want our part of the gold. To build us a future, suh. We've had enough of war. And, like it or not, suh, you'll have to reconcile yourself to that. As far as we're concerned, the fighting is over."

"Shelby will fight on," Rhett said.

McGregor shrugged. "That's *your* opinion, Cap'n. And all of us owe you thanks for us getting the gold. But even if Shelby fights, we've no intention of joining him. Please understand that, suh. With all due respect, we're each going our own way as of when we cross the river."

"I say you're not."

"Be reasonable, suh. We'd all rather part on good terms. And, like I said, you can't fight us all. You can take your own share to Shelby, if you're determined to do so."

"My share won't finance an army," Rhett said.

"You'll have a double share, suh. We've agreed on that. You'll have Corporal Hall's share, besides your own."

"Still not enough for Shelby's plan."

"And better that it isn't, suh. There's been four years of killing, suh. We've even come to killing our own southern boys, these last few days. The war has driven us all mad, suh. Only peace will restore our sanity."

"Do you think gold will do it?"

McGregor's serious expression broke into a faint, wry grin. "We figure it'll help, suh. We surely do." He paused, and turned serious again. "Begging your pardon, suh, but I think you have been driven a little more mad than the rest of us. Take your share and look to your own life, Cap'n. Don't trust some hotspur general with your gold."

"General Shelby is to be trusted."

"Suh, nobody is to be trusted. Not when it comes to gold." McGregor's grin widened. "We are a prime example of that."

He raised his arm suddenly and signaled the others to follow him, and rode down the bank of the river and began splashing across it. He did not look back.

The rest of the rebels rode up in single file. Each twisted in his saddle as he came abreast of Rhett and saluted sharply before plunging into the water.

Rhett stared at them, his face granite-hard and expressionless. He did not return their salutes.

After they had passed, he sat there a long time.

Thinking.

He was still there when a horseman came across the river toward him. He watched the approaching figure with disinterested, listless eyes, all the sap gone out of him.

When the stranger was within hailing distance, Rhett saw the worn gray uniform, and his interest rose. He was curious that the man did not shy off at the sight of Rhett's own Union blue.

He was more surprised when he recognized the rider.

The man in gray grinned. "Some of your men told me you might still be here," he said. "You remember me, suh?"

"Cameron, isn't it?" Rhett said. "Lieutenant Cameron."

"That's right, suh. One of Shelby's Iron Brigade."

"What are you doing here, Cameron?"

"Going back to Texas, to take my chances, suh. Big mistake in running off."

"Mistake?"

"Following Shelby the way we did. Can't blame him entirely, though. Things just didn't work out the way he figured down there in Mexico."

"He's still going to carry on the fight, isn't he?"

"No, suh, he sure isn't. Maximilian wouldn't let us base there as a military force. Old Max is bent on getting diplomatic recognition by the U.S.A., not in helping their enemy. The best he'd let us do, is to become farmers way to hell and gone down near Veracruz."

"Shelby settled for that?"

"Didn't have much choice, I guess. No way the North is going to give him amnesty now, him having talked so big about never surrendering." Cameron paused. "Him and Price and some other generals and colonels are stuck there."

"And you?"

"Hell, suh, who is going to recognize me, a plain unknown soldier? I figure I can blend in with several thousand others like me, and take up where I left off. The U.S.A. can't punish all of us. They wouldn't have time to get on with what they got to do. It's the bigwigs that are stuck."

The bigwigs, and the marked men like himself, Rhett thought bitterly. The dream had exploded, and his part in trying to make it work had made him a wanted man. There'd be no amnesty for him. Not when they suspected he had a part in the disappearance of the gold.

"There's others like me heading back home," Cameron said. "Me, I'm a Texan like yourself, suh. I'm going back." He paused. "I met your men on the other side and they told me what your original intentions were. Well, suh, I'm telling you the way it is now, and that's the God's truth." He paused again. "If you're of a mind, I'd be proud to have you ride with me."

Rhett was silent, pondering. Finally, he said, "Thanks, but I reckon not. As you see, and the men no doubt told you, I'm a Galvanized Yankee, which means I'm a deserter from the Union Army, not the Confederate. They'll shoot me if they pick me up."

Cameron thought about this. "I guess that's so, suh. Well, I wish you luck, whatever you do." He gave a lax salute, nodded, and rode off in the direction of the trail to San Antonio.

It was gone. The goal he had lived for all these months was gone. Rhett was faced with hard decisions. Like Cameron, he had no desire to raise crops in Mexico. Cattle, maybe. But Mexico had its own share of cattle barons, the big and powerful *hacendados*.

Texas? No, they'd be looking for him there. New Mexico? Still too close, maybe, but possible. Arizona?

California? The Pacific Coast had stayed pretty well out of the conflict, isolated by the barrier of empty land. Hell, he remembered he now had a fortune in his saddlebags. He felt a resurgence of hope. He'd go to California, take his chances there.

He'd keep the gold. He'd paid his price for it. And now that he felt betrayed by exiled generals and colonels, he'd not turn it over to them to squander on themselves.

He'd do as McGregor and the others proposed to do. Use his share to build a future.

And suddenly a vision of Sherry came to him, and he was taken by a longing so strong he wanted to cry out.

How could he reach her?

The answer would have disheartened him, had not his long-repressed desire flared into hot determination. He'd have to retrace the trail he'd just taken down from the north. Close to a thousand miles, and now, with a fortune on his saddle and another on a led horse, he was without funds to provision himself for the journey.

He dared not redeem even one of the ingots. It would arouse suspicion, even if he went to San Antonio.

He'd have to live off the country. He'd better hope he'd find enough game to keep him going. His mount and the pack animal were tired from the long trip down. It'd take a while, but he could see no other way.

Weeks later he paused on the fringe of Cheyenne Springs. And here caution held him as he reviewed the possibilities of how he would be received. His past experiences with its Union sympathizers did little for his confidence. Still, he had to somehow get word to Sherry, to let her know he had come back.

And again, uncertainty struck him. How would *she* react?

He gave considerable thought to these questions, and then, abruptly, he turned toward the stage station and came up on it from the south.

He studied his old bivouac area for sign of replacement troops, and was agreeably surprised to see none. He did see Searle, out in the workshop area adjacent to the corral. A couple of his hostlers were with him.

He detoured to the west side of the main station building, and tied up his animals where he hoped they would not be seen. He watched briefly, then slipped in through the front door.

He felt a quick relief as he discovered no one inside the big room. He heard Esther working in the kitchen.

He stepped through the connecting doorway and spoke her name.

She whirled away from the cook stove and stared with fright. A moment passed before she said, in disbelief, "Justin? Oh my God! What has happened to you?"

It was only then that he remembered he hadn't shaved for weeks, hadn't even bathed since a stream he'd crossed days back, and that his worn uniform was stiff and stinking from sweat and grime and the grease of trail-cooked wild game.

He felt ashamed, and started to draw back away from her.

But she would have none of that. She rushed toward him and put her hands on his arms and held him. Nothing more, just that, and he wondered, as he had wondered so many weeks before, at the strange feeling she seemed to have for him.

"Oh, God! Justin, I'm so glad to see you—alive! But you shouldn't have come back."

"I had to, ma'am."

"*Esther.*"

"I had to, Esther."

"Why?"

There was an eager hopefulness in her voice that kept him from answering. There was a light in her eyes.

As the silence lengthened, he saw the light go out. Her hands loosened, though she still held him lightly.

She said then, "It's Sherry, isn't it? You came back for Sherry."

He nodded, almost afraid to do so.

"Of course you did," she said. And then, peculiarly, some of the light seemed to return to her eyes. "And you want me to fetch her to you."

"Would you?"

"Yes," she said. "I'll do that for you, Justin. Oh, you *knew* I would."

"No, ma'am. But I was hoping."

"You can't wait here. There are people about. Union

officers sometimes. Is there a place by the river, a trysting place perhaps, where you might meet her?"

Somewhat sheepishly, he said, "Yes. Yes, there is."

"Go there and wait. I'll send her to you."

"I ought to clean up some," he said.

"No! Not now!" A harshness was in her voice. "If she is your woman, she'll accept you as you are."

"Still—"

"Do as I say, or I'll not send her."

"I guess I have no choice."

"You don't," Esther said.

He waited at the spot where they had once made love.

But first he plunged into the river shallows, clothes and all, and let the sluggish current cleanse him as it could. He came out refreshed, if soaked, and felt the hot, stirring breeze begin to dry him.

He was still quite damp when she arrived, walking rapidly, and burst into their hidden clearing. She stopped at the sight of him, taken aback by his appearance even as Esther had been.

She said, "Justin! Is it you?"

He wanted to go to her, but he held himself back, giving her the choice. She did not move, just kept staring at him, until in exasperation he said, "Yes, it's me."

"Why did you come back?"

"For you."

"What happened in Mexico?"

"I didn't cross."

"Why?"

He couldn't tell her the truth. Not now. If he did, he knew he'd lose her. There were some things better left unsaid. Even to himself, his earlier reasoning and his blind commitment to the lost cause seemed a foolish mistake. Loyalty could do that to a man; he knew that now.

He said, "I realized I wanted you above all else."

She still did not move. "I still think about Lyle when I'm lonely. After you left, almost every night. Would it be fair to you, Justin?"

"I want you, Sherry, no matter what."

"I was hurt when you left."

"I know."

"You can't stay here. The people are grateful for what you did. But to the army you'll be a deserter, you know that."

"I know."

"What will you do?"

"Will you go with me?"

"Where?"

"We'll find a place."

"You will never be safe. Anywhere."

"Nobody is ever safe," he said. "But the West is big. Will you take a chance with me?"

She began to slowly move toward him, her eyes on his face. She stopped within reach of his embrace and waited.

He took her in his arms then, and held her close.

"Yes," she said. "Yes, Justin. I will, if you'll take the chance with me."

If you have enjoyed this book and would like to receive details of other Walker Western titles, please write to:

Western Editor
Walker and Company
720 Fifth Avenue
New York, NY 10019